Ralph Bennett

AS HERC TURNED, HE WAS CERTAIN THAT HE HAD SEEN A FACE VANISH QUICKLY FROM THE CASEMENT.

—Page 62

THE DREADNOUGHT BOYS ON AERO SERVICE

BY
CAPTAIN WILBUR LAWTON

AUTHOR OF "THE DREADNOUGHT BOYS ON BATTLE PRACTICE," "THE DREADNOUGHT BOYS ABOARD A DESTROYER," THE DREADNOUGHT BOYS ON A SUBMARINE," ETC.

NEW YORK
HURST & COMPANY
PUBLISHERS

Copyright, 1912,
BY
HURST & COMPANY

CONTENTS

CHAPTER		PAGE
I.	Something New in Naval Life	5
II.	"If He's a Man, He'll Stand Up"	17
III.	For the Trophy of the Fleet	30
IV.	The Aero Squad	39
V.	Uncle Sam's Men-birds	50
VI.	Ned Invents Something	59
VII.	A Rescue by Aeroplane	73
VIII.	Herc Gets a "Talking To"	84
IX.	A Conspiracy is Ripening	93
X.	A Dreadnought Boy at Bay	103
XI.	In Their Enemies' Hands	113
XII.	"Stop Where You Are!"	123
XIII.	Harmless as a Rattlesnake	136
XIV.	Flying for a Record	148
XV.	A Drop From Space	156
XVI.	The Setting of a Trap	167
XVII.	The Springing Thereof	178

CONTENTS

CHAPTER		PAGE
XVIII.	ON BOARD THE SLOOP	190
XIX.	"BY WIRELESS!"	200
XX.	NED, CAST AWAY	213
XXI.	A STRIKE FOR UNCLE SAM	223
XXII.	SOME ADVENTURES BY THE WAY	233
XXIII.	"YOU ARE A PRISONER OF THE GOVERNMENT!"	243
XXIV.	A DASH FOR FREEDOM	255
XXV.	THE MYSTERIOUS SCHOONER—CONCLUSION	267

The Dreadnought Boys on Aero Service

CHAPTER I.

SOMETHING NEW IN NAVAL LIFE.

One breezy day in early June, when a fresh wind off shore was whipping the water into sparkling white caps, excitement and comment fairly hummed about the crowded foredecks of the big Dreadnought *Manhattan*.

The formidable looking sea-fighter lay with half a dozen other smaller naval vessels—battleships and cruisers—in the stretch of water known as Hampton Roads, which, sheltered by rising ground, has, from time immemorial, formed an anchorage for our fighting-ships, and is as rich in historical associations as any strip of sea within the jurisdiction of the United States.

The cause of all the turmoil, which was agitating every jackie on the vessel, was a notice which had been posted on the ship's bulletin board that morning.

It was tacked up in the midst of notices of band concerts, challenges to boxing matches, lost or found articles, and the like. At first it had not attracted much attention. But soon one jackie, and then another, had scanned it till, by means of the thought-wireless, which prevails on a man-of-war, the whole fore part of the ship was now vibrant and buzzing with the intelligence.

The notice which had excited so much attention read as follows:

"Enlisted Men and Petty Officers: You are instructed to send your volunteer applications for positions in the experimental Aero squad. All applications to be made in writing to Lieutenant De Frees in charge of the experiment station."

"Aero service, eh?" grunted more than one grizzled old shell-back, "well, I've served my time in many an old sea-going hooker, but hanged if I'd venture my precious skin on board a sky-clipper."

"Aye, aye, mate. Let the youngsters risk their lily-white necks if they want to," formed the burden of the growled responses, "but you and me 'ull smoke Uncle Sam's baccy, and take our pay with a good deck under our feet."

But this state of caution did not extend to the younger members of the ship's company. Least of all to Boatswain's Mate Herc—otherwise Hercules—Taylor and his inseparable chum, Ned Strong, the latter of whom was now chief gunner's mate of the biggest vessel in the navy.

Neither Ned nor Herc smoked. By observation of those who did indulge in the practice, they had discovered that the use of tobacco affected more senses than one, and rendered a man incapable of the highest physical proficiency. The custom of smoking not only impaired the eyesight of many a gunner, but in the athletic sports, of which both lads were so fond, it also showed its bad effects. Ned knew of more than one promising young gun-pointer who had been compelled to relinquish his laurels on account of tobacco-affected eyesight.

As a consequence, the two trim, clean-cut lads, their faces bronzed and clear from sea air and clean living, stood apart from the group about the "smoke-lamp."

"I'm going to send in my name," announced Ned with twinkling eyes. "The aero section of the navy is going to be an important one in the future. There is a good chance for a chap to advance himself in such work."

"By the great horn spoon!" muttered Herc, in his enthusiastic, whimsical way, "I'm with you, Ned. We'll be regular sky-pilots before the summer's out!"

He began to rub his shoulder-blades, while a humorous smile played over his freckled, straightforward features.

"What's the matter?" asked Ned, noting Herc's brisk rubbing of the part aforesaid.

"Oh, hum! I thought I felt my wings sprouting," replied Herc, with a broad grin.

"Tell you what, we've a few minutes yet. Let's get our ditty boxes—or 'ditto' boxes, as you used to call them—and write our applications at once."

"Let's talk a while longer," said Herc, with an odd look.

"Why, what's the matter? Surely you aren't regretting your determination already."

Herc, for reply, bent over and touched his feet.

"No; they're not cold," he said; "I thought for a minute they were." Then he looked up into the cloudless blue vault of the heavens.

"Say, Ned, it's an awful long way up there, isn't it? How far, I wonder?"

"What do you want to know for?" asked Ned, moving away.

"Oh, nothing. Only I'd like to know how far we are likely to tumble, in case we get our applications accepted, and in case we fly as high as the sky, and in case——"

"Oh, come on, Herc," urged Ned; "time enough to worry about that when we are assigned to aero duty."

"All that goes up must come down," said Herc sagely, joining Ned nevertheless, "but we've reversed the process."

"How do you make that out?"

"Well, when we were on submarine duty we explored the bottom of the sea, didn't we? And now, if all goes well, we're going to venture aloft."

Ned burst into a laugh, and they moved off arm in arm, exchanging greetings with the crowd of blue jackets lounging about at the after-dinner rest. As they threaded their way among them, Herc burst into song:

"'There's a sweet little cherub that sits up aloft!' That's me, Ned."

"First freckled cherub I ever heard of," chuckled Ned.

Leaving the two lads to write their letters, we feel that it is now our duty to let our readers know something more about Ned Strong and Herc Taylor. They are two lads worth knowing. Neither of them much over eighteen years of age, they had, during their short career in the navy, each made his mark in no uncertain fashion. In his chosen branch of the service, Ned Strong was admired by the officers and adored by the men. His advance had been rapid, and some of his more enthusiastic friends were already hinting at a commission in sight for him in the time to come.

As for the merry, light-hearted Herc Taylor, that befreckled youth had as many friends among officers and men as Ned, and was one of the youngest bos'un's mates in the navy.

As readers of the Dreadnought Boys series know, both lads had entered the navy, like so many other "likely" recruits, from a farm. From the first a measure of luck had been theirs. But dogged perseverance, and a determination to overcome all obstacles by honorable means, had, also, aided them not a little in their rapid advance.

In *"The Dreadnought Boys on Battle Practice,"* we followed the early steps of their life in the navy. It was not all as pleasant as they had imagined it would be. To the boys, as "rookies," much hard, and not over-pleasant work, fell. But scrubbing decks, cleaning paint and the like, they accepted in good part. "It's helping to keep our $5,000,000 home trim and fit," was the way Ned used to put it.

A ship's bully tried his best to make their paths thorny, but Ned, in a battle that will live long in forecastle annals, bested him. Kennell tried to take a despicable revenge. With a gang of rascals, he concerned himself in a plot to injure the Dreadnought Boys. But his machinations came to naught. Instead, Ned became the means of saving the inventor of a new explosive and type of gun from a serious predicament. Right after this, Herc's turn came, when he displayed wonderful heroism following a disastrous "flare-back."

Following the stirring days at Guantanamo, came a voyage on a torpedo-boat destroyer, the celebrated *Beale*. The two lads, on this cruise, found themselves plunged into the very thick of a South American revolution. The uprising seriously affected American interests, and, by a stroke of good fortune, our lads were able to play a prominent part in bringing the situation to a successful outcome. In this book one of the many exciting adventures described was the lads' escape from a prison, when it was shelled during a hot engagement, and their subsequent daredevil dash on board a revolutionary torpedo craft.

By this time, although, of course, their participation in the revolution could not be "mentioned in the despatches," the boys had placed themselves in line for promotion. The eyes of their superiors were on them. But success did not spoil them or "swell their heads." They were still just as ready to fulfill an order promptly and cheerfully as in their apprentice days. As that is the spirit that wins in the navy, the Dreadnought Boys were singled out for some hazardous work on board a new type of submarine. Enemies of Uncle Sam nearly succeeded in sinking the diving boat for good and all with an infernal machine, but the boys providentially discovered the plot in time, and saved many lives. In that book, too, they had an interesting encounter with Sound pirates, and played a rather prominent part in the pretty romance of the diving boat's inventor.

The opening of this book finds them back on regular duty. Although the routine of battleship life in times of peace may seem tame and humdrum, the boys, nevertheless, devoted themselves to it with the same cheerful zest which had carried them through so many dashing adventures.

But the quiet and monotonous daily existence which they had enjoyed during and since the winter cruise to European stations, was not to last long. Although they did not know it, the Dreadnought Boys were on the brink of some most remarkable happenings.

"By the way," said Herc, as, their letters written and deposited in the ship's post-office, the two chums emerged on deck once more, "you haven't let this aerial business drive the recollection of to-morrow's races out of your mind, have you?"

He referred to some contests ashore, which had been arranged with enthusiasm by the officers and crews of the ships of the squadron.

"I should say not," laughed Ned. "Why?"

"Nothing, only there are a few chaps in the fleet who'd like to see us both fall down hard. You're in good trim, Ned?"

"I think so. Feel fit, anyway."

"I needn't have asked you. I know you're always in good shape."

"I can return the compliment," laughed Ned.

Just then the bugles began singing the calls for the busy afternoon's practice-work on guns and at drill. With a hasty word, the chums separated and hurried to take their places in the big machine of which they were already important cogs.

CHAPTER II.

"IF HE'S A MAN, HE'LL STAND UP."

The passage of Ned and Herc from the foredeck in quest of their ditty-boxes had not gone unnoted by two men lounging at ease under the shadow of the great 13-inch guns projecting from the forward turret. The big circular steel structure acted as a wind-break, and the pair lay here smoking and talking in low tones.

"I'd give fifty dollars to know Ned Strong's secret," observed one of them, flicking the ashes from a cigar upon the spotless decks, a deliberate infraction of the ship's laws. Selden Merritt was one of the few "before the mast" men on board who smoked cigars. A pipe and a plug of black, rank tobacco usually does for your jackie, but Merritt was an exception to the rule.

"It would be worth it," agreed his companion,

a heavily-set chap of about nineteen. His cap was off, and his black, bristly hair, cut pompadour, stood straight up from his rather low forehead.

Merritt was a man of about twenty-four, blonde, thin and "race-horsey" in build. He had the reputation of having been a college man and champion runner, until, losing prestige and reputation through dissipation, he had been forced to enlist. It had proved the best thing he ever did. Four years in the navy had given him a pink, clear skin, a bright eye and an erect carriage. But it had not taken a furtive sneer out of his expression, nor altered his disposition, which was mean and crafty. His bearing, however, was rather distinguished, with a certain swagger, and his talk showed that he was an educated man.

"Did you have much to do with them on their first cruise?" inquired Merritt's companion, Ray Chance.

"No, they were both enlisted men. But they

managed to give a black eye, in a figurative way, to a good friend of mine."

"You mean Bill Kennell?"

"Yes. I hear that he's been pardoned from prison—political pull. But that doesn't alter the fact that they accomplished his downfall."

"Well, I never liked either of them. I heard about them by reputation before I came to the *Manhattan* from the *Dixie*. I like them still less from what I've seen of them on board here. I think this fellow Strong is a big faker."

"Yes. I'm sick and disgusted with him and the airs he gives himself. His dear chum and inseparable is almost as bad. I'd like to take a fall out of both of them."

"You'll get your chance to-morrow in the squadron's games. You can beat Ned Strong running the best day he ever stepped on a track."

"I ought to be able to, and I mean to do it, too. I don't like bluffs, and this chap Strong is a false alarm if ever there was one."

"Say, you fellows," suddenly interpolated a

voice, "if you think Strong is such a bluff, why don't you tell him so?"

The interruption came from a short, stocky, little blue-jacket, lounging nearby. He had been reading a book on gunnery, but the raised voices of the Dreadnought Boy's detractors had aroused his attention. His blue eyes twinkled rather humorously, as he eyed the agile, long-limbed Merritt and his sallow, dark-haired companion.

"Hullo, Benjamin Franklin; were you rubbering on our conversation?" said Merritt, assuming an indignant expression.

"Ben Franklin" was the nickname given to the studious tar whose right name was Stephen Wynn.

"It didn't take any 'rubbering,' as you call it, to overhear you," said Wynn quietly; "if you take my advice, when you want to say mean things about Ned Strong or his chum, you'll lower your voice aboard this ship. They've got quite a few friends."

"Just the same," maintained Merritt, "the chap

isn't all he sets up to be. He's got some secret, like all such fellows."

"I guess his secret is hard work and attention to duty," said Wynn rather shortly, returning to his reading.

"You don't seriously think that there is any chance of Strong's giving you a tussle for the first place?" asked Ray Chance.

"Frankly, I don't. But there is always a possibility of mistaking one's man. I'm wise enough to know that."

"But you have arranged in some way to make success certain?"

Merritt gave Chance a quizzical look.

"You know me," he said, with a knowing wink, "Chalmers of the old *Luzzy* (sailor slang for the *Louisiana*) is an old friend of mine. He dislikes Strong as much as I do. He's the next best man in the race. If things go wrong, we've got a little system arranged to pocket friend Strong. But how about you? You are pitted against Taylor in the pole vault, aren't you?"

"Yes, and I ain't worrying, you bet."

Merritt still retained a good choice of diction, a relic of his college days, but Chance's talk was was more uncouth and less polished.

"Good! I don't mind telling you I've got some money out on myself. Enough to swamp a good deal of my pay, in fact. I've got to win."

"About the same thing here," grinned Chance; "if I lose, it's all up with me financially. I'm in pretty deep."

"Tell you what," said Merritt suddenly, "I hear that there will be extra pay and bonuses attaching to this aero duty. Let's send in applications, and then if we get trimmed in the races and jumps we will have a chance to get some extra coin."

"That's a good idea," agreed Chance. But as they started to carry out their intention, the same bugle calls that had hastened the steps of Ned and Herc recalled them to duty.

Stephen Wynn arose with a sigh, and thrust his book inside his loose blouse. "Ben Franklin" disliked to leave his studies for duty. But he was a smart sailor, and formed one of Ned's gun crew. Merritt and Chance were on one of the after turrets.

"Those fellows took care to sink their voices after they found out I'd overheard them," said Wynn to himself, as he fell in with the rest of the blue-jackets. "I'll bet that they were plotting some mischief to Strong and Taylor. At any rate, I'll put them on their guard at the first opportunity I get."

At three-thirty, or seven bells, the gun drills and calisthenic exercises were over, and a brief space of leisure ensued. Wynn, according to his determination, sought out Ned and Herc. He lost no time in communicating his suspicions to them. But, somewhat to his astonishment, neither of the lads seemed much impressed.

"A fellow who plots and backbites in dark corners is not one to be scared of," said Ned. "But just the same, Ben Franklin, I'm obliged to you. I guess we'll keep our eyes on our two friends, eh, Herc?"

"Not worth bothering with," observed Herc, "as the car conductor said when the fellow offered him a plugged dime. If they can win fair and square, we won't grudge it to them."

"Well, I've warned you," said "Ben Franklin." "By the way, what makes those fellows so sore at you?"

"Oh, Merritt, so I've heard, was a friend of Bill Kennell. He was the fellow, you know, who kidnapped Mr. Varian in Cuba. He naturally dislikes us for the part we played in apprehending Kennell. As for Chance, he was in my gun crew up to a few weeks ago. I had to have him up 'at the stick' for insubordination once or twice, and I guess it's stuck in his craw."

"If it hadn't been for you, Ned, he'd have gone to the brig," put in Herc.

"Oh, well, I thought that a taste of the brig would be too severe," said Ned. "I hoped a good wigging by the 'old man' (the captain) would be sufficient, but it wasn't. Then Chance sulked and played sick. He took in the doctor for a while, but it didn't last. He was punished and restored to duty with an after gun crew following that."

"And blames you for all his troubles," said Herc indignantly, "and I guess I come in for a share of his dislike."

"Oh, life's too short to worry about Merritt and Chance," said Ned, breaking off the conversation. "It looks as if we'd have a glorious day to-morrow," he went on, adroitly turning the topic of talk. The ruse succeeded. The three shipmates fell to discussing the coming games. Others joined them, and the time passed rapidly till five-thirty,—three bells—when all hands were piped to supper, a plain but substantial meal. For the benefit of our non-seafaring reader, we will tell him that on this particular night it consisted of:—hot roast-beef hash, cold boiled ham, canned peaches, bread, butter and tea or coffee. Thus, it will be seen that Uncle Sam does not starve his blue-jackets.

Supper was in full swing when Ned, who was at the head of the table which seated his "mess," was the recipient of a surprising testimonial.

It came in the shape of a hot baked potato, flung with accuracy and speed. It struck the Dreadnought Boy in the eye, and burst, spreading its pasty contents over his features. Herc, who sat by Ned, leaped to his feet in a flash, while Ned hastily pawed the mass out of his eyes.

"I saw who threw that," cried Herc, his face aflame, the freckles looming up like spots on the sun; "if he's a man, he'll stand up."

A stir ran through the forecastle. Herc's finger pointed to a distant table and rested on the form of Merritt. Chance sat by him. Both had been laughing an instant before, but as Merritt saw that he had been found out his face assumed a rather sickly grin.

"Sit down, Herc," ordered Ned rather sternly, "I'll attend to this. Am I to understand that you threw that potato?" he demanded, fixing his gaze straight on Merritt's face.

The other's eyes sank. He looked disturbed and a bit scared. Ned's voice had held no uncertain ring.

"It—it was just a joke," he said. "You don't need to get huffy about it."

"Rather a strenuous joke, wasn't it?" asked Ned in a firm, calm voice, while the eyes of every man in the place were fixed on him in breathless attention.

"I—I didn't mean to hit you," went on Merritt. "I just wanted to give you a jump. It was just a joke—that's all."

"That being the case," resumed Ned, "I shall have to ask you to remove the consequences of your *joke*."

So saying, he deliberately threw the remains of the potato on the deck.

"Now, come here and pick that up and carry it back," he said, with a flash in his eyes. "We'll carry this joke through to its conclusion."

Merritt turned pale and hesitated. Then he caught Ned's eye. A certain glint in it seemed to galvanize him into action. Amid a roar of laughter from the entire assemblage, Merritt, red and white by turns, crossed to Ned's table and carefully picked up every scrap of the débris.

"What are you laughing at?" he glared at Herc, as he made his way back to his own place.

"At your joke," sputtered Herc, affecting a spasm of amusement. "Ho! ho! ho! That's one of the best jokes I've ever seen."

"It is, is it?" glowered Merritt.

"Yes, but it isn't as big a joke as it would have been if you hadn't done as Ned told you. Ho! ho! ho! It isn't every puppy that will fetch and carry at the first lesson."

The shout of laughter was taken up by the rest of the blue-jackets. Amid this storm of merriment, Merritt made his way to his seat. He reached it just as the officer of the deck entered.

"Merritt, what are you out of your place for?"

demanded this dignitary, who was noted as a strict disciplinarian.

"I—I dropped a potato, sir, and was picking it up," stammered Merritt, trembling with rage and mortification.

CHAPTER III.

FOR THE TROPHY OF THE FLEET.

As Ned had prophesied, the next day was bright and clear. There was just enough of the coolness of early summer to give a crisp tang to the air. It stirred the blood like martial music. It was a day which challenged every athlete in the squadron to do his best. That is, so far as external conditions were concerned.

The ground selected for the trying out of the championship of the squadron was a flat field, some five acres in extent, not far from the shore. It stood on slightly rising ground. Trees, fresh and green, stood in a thick mass on one side. Seaward the ground sloped gently, and beyond could be seen the grim sea-fighters, swinging at anchor; from some of the smoke-stacks vapor curled lazily. The basket-like fighting masts resembled the work of some geometrically inclined spider.

Cheering and laughing, the contingents from the various ships were landed after dinner. In their midst, guarding them jealously, as bees would their queen, each ship's company surrounded their group of athletes. And a fine showing they made when they assembled in the dressing-rooms under the grandstand. This structure was already occupied by the officers of the division, headed by Rear Admiral Cochran, a white-haired veteran of the seven seas. A sprinkling of ladies in bright costumes lent a dash of color to the scene.

The course had been laid out, and the officers who had constituted themselves a committee in charge of the sports were already busy about it, when the *Manhattan's* boats landed their laughing, singing, cheering blue-jackets. Among them were Ned and Herc. Neither of them had yet changed to their running togs. Merritt and Chance had, however, but they both wore long raincoats, which prevented Ned from sizing them up, as he was anxious to do.

Both the Dreadnought Boys were quiet and self-contained as usual. But Merritt and Chance were talking loudly and flinging remarks right and left. Atwell, Turner, Simpkins, Jessup and a dozen other *Manhattan* entries in various events formed the remainder of the athletic contingent from the big dreadnought. As they entered the dressing-rooms—or rather the big space under the grandstand—a babel of cries of welcome and jocular defiance surged about the Manhattanites.

"Here come the champions of the squadron," shouted some one.

"Say, Jack, wait till they are champions before you start giving the title to them," hailed another voice. It was that of Chalmers of the *Louisiana*. He wore dark-green running trunks with a white shirt. Across his chest was a red, white and blue sash, on which was blazoned the name of his ship. Several of the other runners and athletes affected this touch of dandyism. Ned and Herc, however, wore plain running suits: trunks and sleeveless shirts and good track shoes.

Chalmers lost no time in seeking out Merritt. The two conversed in a corner in low tones. After a time, Ned and Herc, too, succeeded in getting away from a crowd of their shipmates and found time to pass a word or two.

Merritt had cast off his long coat to adjust his trunks. Ned found his eyes riveted on the fellow. If physique were any criterion, Merritt should have been a fine runner.

Clean-cut as a race-horse, his skin was smooth and of good color, with lithe muscles playing under it. He was the beau ideal in build of a speed machine. Chance, on the other hand, was heavier-set, but he showed up well in that assemblage of athletically built men and youths. Both Ned and Herc agreed that the two whom they instinctively regarded as enemies were by no means to be rated lightly.

But a sharp bugle call cut short further observation. The games were beginning. The hundred-yard dash was third on the program, and Ned did not emerge till just before the starting time. The wind was sharp, and he did not want to contract his muscles by letting the cold air blow on his limbs. Herc, in a heavy navy coat, went to the starting line with him. He stood by his chum, giving him some last words of advice. Ned appeared to listen, but his thoughts were actually elsewhere. He had already made up his mind to his course of action. He was going to run a waiting race, depending on a sharp spurt to win.

In a quick glance over the six entrants, he saw that Chalmers and Merritt were the only ones he had cause to fear. He noticed them whispering together, and resolved to keep a sharp lookout on their actions.

The air was filled with shouts and suggestions and greetings from blue-jackets, who were encouraging the men from their own ship. Every man in the squadron who could be spared was there. They made a big throng, lining the track on the side away from the grandstand.

"Hey, there, Springer! Do your prettiest for the *Merrimac.*"

"Oh, you Polthew! Don't forget the *Massachusetts!*"

"Say, Polly, look out for that *Manhattan* bunch."

"Hi, Chalmers, you're the man. You're carrying the *Luzzy's* money."

"That's right, and don't you forget it."

"And you, Strong! My month's pay's on you."

"You'll lose, then; Merritt's the man."

"What's the matter with Carter? Guess you'll know there's a *Kansas* in the fleet."

"Stand back, please! Stand back!" cried those in charge of the course.

The line-up was quickly arranged. The starters crouched ready to dart off. Carter made a false start, and the excitement waxed furious.

"Ready?"

Lieutenant Steedforth, of the *Louisiana,* the starter, put the question.

Like greyhounds preparing to leave the leash, the contestants flexed their muscles.

The starter lifted the pistol. A puff of smoke and sharp report followed.

Merritt, Chalmers and Polthew got off at the same instant. They made a showy start, and the grandstand as well as the field buzzed with enthusiasm.

Springer, of the *Merrimac,* and Carter, of the *Kansas,* came next. Strong came last, and was almost unnoticed in the frenzy of excitement.

The pace was terrific. In the first twenty-five yards Polthew and Carter dropped behind, hopelessly out of it. Far in front, Merritt, Chalmers and Springer were fighting it grimly out. Springer hung like death on the heels of the two leaders.

Ned had crept up, and kept his pace steadily. Suddenly Springer spurted. This carried him past Chalmers and Merritt, who were about even. But the effort had been made too soon. In a second's time he dropped back again.

The Dreadnought Boy knew that the two tricksters in front were going to concentrate on stopping him if he crept up too soon. So he crawled up till he felt it would be foolish to delay longer. Then, letting out all his reserve power, Ned spurted. His burst of speed was easy and genuine. It was not forced.

In a flash he was abreast of Chalmers before the latter could "pocket" him according to prearranged plans. Merritt, as he saw this, exerted every ounce of strength in his wiry body.

The jackies went wild. It was anybody's race, for now Chalmers had recovered from his surprise. Spurting, he caught up with the leaders. Spurt followed spurt. The air vibrated with cheers, yells, whoops and every kind of noisy demonstration.

Above it all, there suddenly rang out from the

throats of the *Manhattan's* crew, one ear-splitting cry of triumph.

In the midst of it, carried on its wings as it were, Ned suddenly dashed ahead of his competitors and staggered across the tape into the arms of his shipmates. Chalmers was second and Merritt a bad third. Tobacco had found the weak spot in his heart. He was almost exhausted as he reeled across the line.

CHAPTER IV.

THE AERO SQUAD.

One by one the other contests were decided. The hammer throw was won by Melvin, of the *Idaho,* a giant of a man. Smithers, of the *Manhattan,* was second in this event. So the Dreadnought's crew continued to keep up their spirits. The half-mile was captured by Remington, of the *Louisiana,* while the mile went to Hickey, of the *Manhattan,* a man with hair of right good fighting red, and a great chest development.

Then came the pole jump. As usual, this picturesque event excited great interest.

Chance came first, and set a mark that made the other contestants gasp.

"You'll have to be a grasshopper to beat that, Herc," whispered Ned.

Herc nodded. "I'll do my best," he said simply.

"That's the stuff, shipmate," said "Ben Franklin," who happened to be close at hand, "as poor Richard said:

> " 'You'll beat the rest;
> If you do your best.' "

"I never saw that in 'Poor Richard' that I can recollect," said Ned, with a laugh.

Steve Wynn looked pained, as he usually did when any of his quotations was questioned as to its accuracy.

"It's in the book some place," he said confidently.

"Well, maybe it is," agreed Ned. "It's good advice, anyhow."

At last came Herc's turn.

Merritt had now been joined by Chance. With set teeth, they stood watching the agile lad from the farm prepare for his preliminary run.

"You want to watch closely now," said Chance, with an unholy grin, "you're going to see something."

"What? You've——"

But a horrified cry from the spectators interrupted the words. Herc had risen gracefully at the bar, and had seemed about to sail over it. Instantly bedlam had seethed about the field.

"Taylor, of the *Manhattan*, wins!"

"Good boy, red-top!"

"Go to it, freckles!"

But in a flash the cries of enthusiasm had been changed to that peculiar sighing gasp that runs through a crowd at a sudden turn to the tragic in their emotions.

As Herc had lifted his body outward to sail over the bar, the pole had suddenly snapped beneath him.

The horrified spectators saw the lad's body hurtled downward. Herc, as he fell, narrowly missed impalement on the jagged, broken end of the pole. But the lad's muscles were under prime control. Even as he fell, he seemed to make a marvelous twist.

The cheers broke forth anew as Herc, instead of landing in a heap, came to earth gracefully on his feet. He had not sustained the least injury, a fact which he soon demonstrated to the judges and other officials of the track who crowded about him.

"I tell you, it's that blamed secret of theirs," growled Chance, turning pale.

"We'd better get out of here," warned Merritt hastily. "Look, they are examining the pole. I imagine that they'll find it was cut."

"I imagine so, too," said Chance, in a low, rather frightened tone, as the unworthy two hastened off. "But they can't prove anything on me," he added defiantly.

In the meantime Herc had selected another pole. He examined it carefully and found it perfect. Bracing himself for the effort of his life, he essayed the jump once more.

He sailed over the bar as gracefully as a soaring sea gull.

"Chance is tied! Taylor's tied him!" yelled the crowd.

"Good boy, Herc," whispered Ned, as Herc

prepared for a fresh effort. "Now this time beat him, and beat him good."

Herc set his teeth grimly. His usually good-natured face held an expression very foreign to it.

"I'll do it," he said. "And then," he added significantly, "I've got another job to attend to."

Flexing his muscles, Herc crouched for an instant. Then he hurled himself at the bar. He cleared it with almost six inches to spare above Chance's hitherto unapproached record.

If the field had known enthusiasm before, it was pandemonium that broke loose now. Like wild-fire, the word had gone about that Herc's pole had been tampered with. The spirit of the Yankee blue-jacket is keen for fair play. A foul trick stirs his blood as nothing else will. If Ned or Herc had breathed their suspicions at that instant, it is likely that, in spite of discipline, it would have gone hard with Merritt and Chance. But Herc sought another way.

That night word ran through the fleet that

Hercules Taylor, of the *Manhattan,* had challenged Chance, of the same ship, to a boxing match, and that Chance had refused. Possibly he anticipated that Herc might lose control of himself and strike out a little harder than is consistent with "sparring." At any rate, from that time on, Chance was rated as "a flunker," which, in the navy, is a very undesirable appellation.

Herc, however, was the idol of the *Manhattan.* His winning of the pole jump had captured the athletic supremacy pennant for the *Manhattan.* It had been the climax of a day of triumphs for the lads of the Dreadnought. From thenceforth the big fighting craft was entitled to float both the athletic pennant and the coveted "Meat Ball," the latter the red flag for the best gunnery. How the meat ball was won at Guantanamo, readers of *"The Dreadnought Boys on Battle Practice"* are aware.

It was on a Monday, a week after the sports, that a line of trim, athletic looking, young blue-jackets were lined up in a field, some ten miles out of Hampton, and in the heart of a rural community. Off, at one side of the meadow, was a row of barn-like structures, painted a dull gray color and numbered. There were six of them.

These sheds housed the aeroplanes with which the experiments for the purpose of selecting a naval "aerial-scout class" were to be conducted. The eyes of the row of aspirants, who had been winnowed from a perfect crop of such applicants, were fixed longingly on the gray barns. They housed, not only the aeroplanes, but the ambitions and hopes of that row of young men— the pick of the squadron.

But there were more than twenty candidates for the scout corps lined up, and only nine would be selected. No wonder that there was anxiety reflected in their eyes, as Lieutenant De Frees and his assistants, Ensigns Walters and Jackson, paced down the row of blue-jackets, putting questions here and there, and weeding out those who were either too heavy or cumbersome for aero work, or else did not give evidence of the keen, hawk-like intellectual faculties that an airman must have. These include the power of instant decision in an emergency, courage of a high order, but not recklessness, and a mind capable of grasping the mechanical qualities of the craft with which they have to deal. As may be imagined, then, the task of the officers was not a simple one.

One by one, the eager applicants were sorted and sifted, till finally, the chosen nine stood shoulder to shoulder. Ned and Herc had both passed, although, for a time, the fate of the latter had hung in the balance. His heavy frame was against him. But the naval officers had decided that the lad's quick intelligence and bull-dog tenacity made him desirable in other ways. For the present Herc Taylor would be held in reserve. There was a certain grim suggestiveness in this—a hint of the dangers of aerial navigation which might result in the ranks being thinned before long.

Ned had had no trouble in getting by. Lieutenant De Frees had said with a pleasant nod:

"I've heard of you, Strong. We want you. You are, of course, willing to sign a paper absolving the navy from responsibility in case of your death or serious injury?"

This question had been put to all the applicants in turn. They had all signified their willingness to do this. It was understood, of course, that the contract, or pledge, did not in any way affect their pensions or "disability" money.

When Ned's turn came, he thought a moment. Such was his habit. Then he spoke.

"If I'd thought only of the risks, sir, I wouldn't be here," he said, in a respectful but decisive manner.

Among the others who passed the ordeal were Merritt and Chance; a slender, greyhound-like chap from the *Kansas,* named Terry Mulligan; a bos'un's mate from the *Louisiana,* called Sim Yeemans, a typical Yankee from

Vermont, or "Vairmont," as he called it; a comical German blue-jacket from the *Idaho*, Hans Dunderblitz, and some others whom we shall probably become acquainted with as our narrative progresses.

The disappointed ones were spun back to the ships in a big auto chartered for the purpose. The successful candidates and the defeated ones parted without animosity.

"Better luck next time," hailed the chosen nine, as their shipmates drove off.

"Oh, your ranks will thin out quick enough," cried one of the departing ones, with sinister humor.

The men selected for the aviation "classes," as they may be called, were, they soon found out, to board at a big stone farmhouse not far from the aviation field. Little more was done that day than to pay a series of visits to the different sheds—or "hangars," in airmen's parlance. In each of these the embryo airmen listened to a short talk on the type of machine they were viewing and heard its qualities discussed. In addition, that night, each of the ambitious ones received a set of books on the science of mastering the air, with instructions to study them carefully. It was implied that those who failed to pass certain examinations at a future date would not be allowed to partake further in the experiments.

"Well, talk about your ease and luxury," said Herc that night when the Dreadnought Boys were in the room assigned to them at the farmhouse, "we're as well off here as middies at Annapolis. What a contrast to the forecastle! I feel like a millionaire already."

"Umph!" grunted Ned, who was already deep in his books. "You'd better get to work and study. We've lots of hard work ahead of us."

"And excitement too, I guess," said Herc, dragging a bulky volume toward him.

Neither of the two lads at the time fully appreciated how much of both was shortly to be crowded into their lives.

CHAPTER V.

UNCLE SAM'S MEN-BIRDS.

"Py golly, dot feller Neddie he fly like vun birdt, alretty, ain'd it?" exclaimed Hans Dunderblitz one day two weeks later.

He was standing by the side of Herc Taylor, watching the evolutions of the bi-plane of Bright-Sturgess model, which Ned Strong was manipulating far above them.

"You're pretty good yourself, Hans," encouraged Herc.

"Ach nein! Efferey time I gedt oop midt der air I schneeze. Undt den—down I go tumble, alretty."

"You'll have to learn to stop sneezing," commented Herc; "maybe the engine doesn't like it— see a doctor."

"Phwat's thot about docthors?" asked Mulligan, coming up. "Shure talkin' uv doctors reminds me uv one we had at home in Galway. He was a successful docthor, understan', but whin he wos a young mon he was not so well-to-do. In fact, the only ornament he had in his parlor was Patience on a Monument, a stathoo, ye understan'. Wun day a frind calls ter see him in the days whin the doc was prosperous.

"'Doc,' says he, 'you ain't got Patience on a Monument any more.'

"'No,' says the docthor, says he, 'shure I've got monumints on all my patients now, begob!'"

"Puts me in mind of what I once read in a paper up in the Catskills," laughed Herc. "The item read: 'Dr. Jones was called, and under his prompt and skilful treatment Hiram Scroggs died Wednesday night.'"

"By Chermany, dere vos a docthor vunce——" began Hans.

But what the doctor "by Chermany" did or said, was destined not to be known, for an order came to the group to resume their practice. Immediately they hastened off to get their machines in trim once more.

Lieutenant De Frees' system of instruction had proved effectual. By this time almost all of his squad had learned to fly. Some of them could only take "grasshopper jumps," but others, Ned, Merritt and Chance among them, had proven themselves really capable airmen. They had learned with wonderful aptitude.

Ned would never forget his first day in an aeroplane. The officer had taken up a biplane and given a daring exhibition. Then he descended and announced that instruction would begin. His assistants took up Herc and Merritt, while Ned was ordered to seat himself on the narrow little place beside the officer. The Dreadnought Boy experienced then, not exactly fear, but a curious sort of sinking feeling born of his initiation into a hitherto unknown experience. He braced his feet against the slender struts of the machine, as he was instructed, and held tightly to the handholds provided for the purpose.

ON AERO SERVICE 53

Then he stole a glance at Lieutenant De Frees. The officer's face was as calm as that of a man who was about to take an afternoon's drive behind a favorite horse.

Suddenly the officer twitched a brass contrivance attached to a quadrant on his steering handle, which was not unlike that of an automobile. He pressed a pedal with his foot and a mighty roar and vibration began at once as the motor opened up.

The acrid reek of castor oil, which is used to lubricate aeroplanes, filled the air. The stuff was expelled from the cylinder vents in blue clouds, shot with lambent smoky flame. The mighty power exerted by the eight cylinders shook the frail fabric of the aeroplane as an earthquake might.

"Hold on tight now!" shouted the officer to the pupils, who were gripping the machine tightly, grasping on to the rear structure. Had they not done so, it would have darted off at once before the two propellers gained top speed and driving power.

"Now!" shouted the officer suddenly.

Instantly they let go, as they had been instructed. Ned felt as if he had suddenly been plunged into a runaway express train that was careening over a newly ploughed field. The shocks and vibration of the machine, as it rushed straight forward, like a scared jackrabbit, over the uneven surface of the field, made it hard to hold on.

Just as Ned felt that he must inevitably be hurled from his seat, the motion suddenly changed. The contrast was violent. From the jouncing, rattling, bumping onrush of a second before, the novice seemed to have been suddenly transported to the softest of feather-beds. The aeroplane glided upward without any apparent effort. It appeared to Ned as if the land was dropping from under his feet, rather than that they were rising from the earth.

Higher they soared and higher. Suddenly

ON AERO SERVICE

their pleasant drifting, as it seemed, though the aeroplane was making sixty miles an hour, changed to a terrifying drop.

It was like rushing downward in a runaway elevator. Ned choked, caught his breath, and turned faint and dizzy. Without wishing to do so, he found himself compelled to close his eyes. The qualms of incipient nausea began to rack him. His head pained, too.

"Gracious," he thought impatiently, "what's the matter with me, anyway? Am I a baby or a girl? If the lieutenant can stand it, I can."

With a supreme effort of will, the Dreadnought Boy compelled himself to open his eyes. He stole a side glance at his companion. Lieutenant De Frees was as cool as an iceberg.

"I must be, too," thought Ned, steeling himself. As he did so, the alarming downward motion ceased. They began to rise once more, swinging upward and climbing the sky in long, lazy circles.

It was then and there that Ned's attack of air

fever left him, never to return. Compared to the experiences of his companions, he learned later he had had a comparatively mild attack.

Ned now began to look about him. The other two aeroplanes were soaring below them, like big birds of the buzzard kind. He felt a wild desire suddenly gripping his heart to go higher—right up among the fleecy clouds that hung above them. Perhaps the officer read his thoughts. At any rate, they continued to climb the aerial staircase. At a height of four thousand feet, they plunged into a fog. The sudden change from the bright sunlight was bewildering.

"We are passing through one of those clouds that you saw from below," volunteered the officer. He glanced at the barograph and read off to Ned the height to which they had arisen.

"Good gracious," thought the lad, "four thousand feet above the earth, and nothing between me and it but the soles of my shoes!"

But Ned's terror had gone. He began to take a real interest in the operation of the aeroplane now. It was fascinating to a degree. All at once they emerged from the wet fog bank and glided into the sunlight. Condensed moisture covered the planes. Drops of water, turned to miniature rainbows by the sunlight, slid down the wire stays and supports.

"Want to go higher?" asked the officer presently.

"If you want to, sir," said Ned.

"We might as well. You are standing it splendidly, Strong."

Ned felt himself glow with pleasure. Words of praise from an officer are not plentiful in our or any other navy. But, as we have seen, the discipline on the aviation squad was not exactly as rigid as on board a battleship.

But presently Ned's pleasant glow gave way to a shivering sensation. It was growing bitterly cold. His teeth chattered and his hands turned a beautiful plum color. The moisture from the cloud began to freeze on the machine.

"Enough for to-day," decided the officer, and he started to descend.

The drop was rapid, yet now that Ned was more used to it, he felt no particular alarm. In an incredibly short time, so it seemed, the earth rushed up to meet them, and they landed on the aviation field as lightly as a wind-wafted feather.

The next day Ned and the two other most proficient pupils—Merritt and Chance—were given a chance to handle the levers alone. They acquitted themselves well. Their advancement proved rapid, living up to the promise of their first efforts. On the day which we described at the beginning of this chapter, Ned, as we have seen, was capable of handling an aeroplane alone. So were Merritt and Chance. Herc was a fair airman, and the others were progressing favorably.

But the real rivals of the air were, at present, Ned, Merritt and Chance.

CHAPTER VI.

NED INVENTS SOMETHING.

"What are you so busy over, my lad?" inquired Lieutenant De Frees one morning, stopping in front of the Dreadnought Boys' hangar.

Ned looked up from the sheet of paper over which he had been poring. It was covered with figures and geometrical scrawlings made by a stumpy lead pencil.

The lad was a bit abashed. Herc was busy tuning up his aeroplane, and Ned, by this time, should have been busy on his machine, for it was a clear, calm day, ideal for a flight. But Ned had not yet even donned his aviation togs. Instead, he had been putting in the best part of an hour on his figuring, bending over it with a puckered brow. A moment before the officer had poked his head in at the door, the boy had started up with a glad cry:

"Herc, I've got it!"

"Catching?" inquired Herc, as he tightened the turnbuckle of a slack stay-wire.

"I hope so," laughed Ned. "I hope it proves catching enough for Uncle Sam to adopt. You see, an aeroplane fitted with pontoons——"

"Oh, choke it off. I've heard it all a hundred times," began Herc, and then, dropping his bantering expression, the freckled lad went on:

"It's a great thing, Ned, not a doubt of it. But are you sure you've got it at last?"

"Certain sure," smiled Ned confidently; "it was to attain cubic capacity, combined with strength and lightness, that bothered me. But I think I've figured it out now so that it will work."

So saying, he had resumed his calculations and had been engaged on them but a few seconds when the interruption occurred.

"Why, it's an idea I've been working out for some time, sir," said Ned modestly, in reply to the officer's question. "I'd rather like to have your opinion on it, sir, if it isn't too much to ask. You see, it's a scheme to attach pontoons to an aeroplane, making the machine practicable for both air and water. Inasmuch as our experiments are to select a naval type, it seemed to me that——"

"A machine that could fly and swim, too, if necessary, would be a great thing," broke in the officer enthusiastically. "Well, my boy, if you really have such an idea in practicable shape, I think I can encourage you to hope great things for it. Any one of a hundred manufacturers would be willing to buy your secret and pay you well for it, too."

Ned flushed. A flicker of something akin to indignation crossed his face.

"If it's any good, sir," he said quietly, "I intended that our navy should have it."

The officer brought down his hand with a hearty slap on Ned's broad shoulder.

"Good for you," he said. "I spoke as I did to test your motives in working on this invention, and I am not disappointed in you. If you will visit me at my quarters to-night, we'll talk more of the matter."

"Thank you, sir," rejoined Ned, flushing gratefully, and his eyes shining, "at what time, sir?"

"About nine o'clock. I've some friends coming over this evening and shall not be at liberty before that time."

Ned saluted, and Herc likewise clicked his heels together and raised his hand, as the officer left the hangar to resume his morning tour of inspection.

The tall form of their superior had hardly vanished from the doorway before Herc, who had turned to search for some tool, gave a sudden sharp outcry.

There was a small window, high up in the rear of the shed, which had been left open for ventilation. As Herc turned, he was as certain as he was that it was daylight, that he had seen a face vanish quickly from the casement. Its owner had evidently dropped from the opening through which he had chosen to spy on the Dreadnought Boys.

"What's up, Herc?" asked Ned, as he caught his chum's smothered exclamation.

"Why—why," exclaimed Herc, "I could be almost certain that I saw the face of Chance vanish from that window as I turned round."

"Eavesdropping, eh?"

"Looks like it. I guess he saw Lieutenant De Frees come in here and remain longer than ordinarily. It must have aroused their curiosity."

"What do you mean by 'they'?"

"Merritt and Chance, of course. You know how much love they bear us. I guess they felt afraid we were stealing a march of some kind on them.

"It's a mean trick!" continued Herc. "If I'd only caught him before I'd—I'd have bust his face."

"Let's go round to the back of the shed. We can soon find out if anyone was really there, or if your imagination played you a trick."

Herc readily agreed. He was fairly boiling with anger. But, on investigation, the fresh paint at the rear of the shed proved not to be scratched, as must have been the case had any one clambered up to the window.

"Looks to me as if you're seeing things," teased Ned.

"Does look rather like it," confessed Herc. "It seems as if—hullo, what—what's that? I guess that's how he reached the window without scratching the paint."

He pointed to a short ladder, evidently left behind by the workmen who had fitted up the hangars. It lay in some tall grass, a short distance from where the Dreadnought Boys stood. A hasty attempt seemed to have been made to hide it, but if this had been the case, it was unsuccessful.

"Just as I thought," declared Herc, after a minute. "The grass here is freshly trampled by the chap who threw the ladder back."

Ned was silent a minute. Then he spoke.

"I wonder how much they overheard?" he said slowly.

"All our conversation, I guess, if they arrived in time. Why?"

"Because I wanted to keep my pontoon idea secret till I'd tried it out. It isn't exactly for general publication—yet."

Herc seemed to catch a deeper meaning in the words.

"You're thinking of that chap who's been snooping around here for the last week posing as a newspaper photographer?" he asked quickly.

"Yes. I'm convinced, somehow, that he is nothing of the sort. For one thing, he's far too curious about the mechanical details of the aeroplanes, and the results of the experiments so far as we've conducted them. Another thing is, that he seems unusually well supplied with money, and he also appears to be a man of far greater ability than his supposed job would indicate."

"Gee whillakers!" gasped Herc. "You're not after thinking he's a foreign spy?"

"That's just what I am," rejoined Ned firmly.

"He won't get much information here."

"Not if he depended on most of us for it. But there's Chance and Merritt. It's a mean thing to say, Herc, but I wouldn't trust those fellows any farther than I could see them, and not so far as that."

"We-el!" whistled Herc, with huge assumed surprise, "you don't say so? I was always under the delusion that they were honest, above-board sports, who wouldn't do a mean thing for all the wealth on Wall Street."

But just then the assembly bugle rang out sharply, summoning the aero squad to its labors. The lads hastened to get their machines out on the field. As they trundled them forth, assisted by some of the men employed about the grounds for such jobs, Ned's machine almost collided with a short, rather thick-set man, with a huge pair of moustaches and luxuriant blonde hair. The latter hung in a tangle from under a battered derby hat. The rest of the man's garments were

Sigmund Muller, free-lance photographer, bore an indescribable air of being something other than he pretended to be.

in keeping with his disreputable head-gear. They consisted of a long, and very greasy-looking frock coat, a pair of checked trousers, badly frayed at the bottoms, broken boots and a soiled shirt and collar.

Over his back was strapped a black leather box, which evidently contained a camera, for under his arm he bore a folded tripod. But, despite his disreputable appearance, Sigmund Muller, free-lance photographer, as he termed himself, bore an indescribable air of being something other than he pretended to be. Ned was skilled in reading human faces, and the first time he had set eyes on Herr Muller, he had decided that under the battered exterior and slouching gait lay hidden a keen, lance-like intellect, and an unscrupulous daring. The lad was impressed with the conviction that here was a man to be reckoned with.

As the advancing aeroplane almost knocked him down, Herr Muller jumped nimbly to one side. Then he assumed what was meant to be a free-and-easy sort of manner.

"Chust for dot," he exclaimed, "I dakes me a picdgure of your aeromoplane. Yes—no?"

He began to unsling his camera, but Ned stopped him in a flash.

"Don't bother yourself," he said sharply. "You recollect that I told you the other day that it was against the rules to take pictures of any of the aeroplanes on the grounds."

"Undt I voss ordered off, too," chuckled Herr Muller, without displaying the slightest trace of irritation, "budt, you see, mein young friendt, I coom back—yah."

"Do you mind standing out of the way?" cut in Herc suddenly. "I'd hate to run you down, but if you stand in the road any longer I'll have to."

Once more Herr Muller jumped nimbly aside.

"Dot'll be all righdt," he said amicably, "go on! Go ahead! Some day you break your neck, undt den I take picdgure of you—yes, no?"

He fixed the freckled-faced boy with a glance

ON AERO SERVICE 69

as he spoke. Herc, despite his usual equanimity, felt a shudder run through him, as he encountered the look. It seemed to penetrate like the white-hot flame of a blow-pipe.

"Whoof!" he exclaimed, as he hastened along, "that chap's about as pleasant a thing to have around as a rattlesnake. He gives me the shivers."

As the Dreadnought Boys hastened to the assembling place, Merritt and Chance, with their machines, emerged. They passed close to Herr Muller, and as they went by he overheard every word they said.

"So Ned Strong is trying to sneak into favor again, eh?" snarled Merritt, who had just been listening to Chance's account of what he had overheard at the hangar window.

"Yes, confound him. I wish we could find some way to put them both out of business. If it wasn't for them, we'd be——"

A soft touch on Chance's arm interrupted him. He faced round and was rather startled to see the shambling figure of Sigmund Muller at his elbow. The man's face bore a peculiar, searching look. Chance felt a sort of shiver run through him as he faced him. But he shook it off.

"Well, what is it?" he demanded gruffly.

"You were talking about Ned Strong and Herc Taylor and some plans they had?" said the photographer in quiet tones.

"Why, y-y-y-yes," stammered Chance, rather taken aback. But then, with a return to his former bravado: "What business have you eavesdropping, anyhow? What business is it of yours, eh?"

The other paid no attention to this outburst.

"You don't like Ned Strong or Herc Taylor?" he said in the same even tone.

"Like them," repeated Chance indignantly, "I should say not, I hate—but what do you want to know for?"

"Because I don't like them either," was the reply. "If you'll meet me at eight o'clock to-night at the old barn, the other side of the stone bridge on the Medford Road, I'll have a proposition of interest to make to you."

"What do you think I am—crazy, as you are?" burst out Chance. "Meet you to talk moonshine? What could you do?"

"Put you in the way of making a lot of money," was the rejoinder.

"Money!" Chance laughed scornfully. "Why, you're nothing but a hobo yourself. If you know where there's so much money, why don't you—— Great Scott!"

Herr Muller had quietly thrust his hand into an inside pocket and withdrawn an immense roll of bills. Chance could see that they were all of big denominations. But he only got a brief look at the roll, for it was almost instantaneously replaced.

"Well," said Herr Muller, with a quiet smile tinged with some contempt, "what do you think of my credentials?"

"They're—they're all right," gasped Chance,

still staring as if fascinated at the shabby figure before him.

"You and your friend will agree, then, that I am worth talking business with?"

The other thought a minute.

"My name's Chance, and I'll take one," he said, as he turned and swiftly hastened off. He had lingered a long time and faced a reprimand. But he took it philosophically, for an idea had occurred to him, a plan which might be the means of freeing himself and his chosen companion from what they deemed the drudgery and hardships of the life of a sailor.

CHAPTER VII.

A RESCUE BY AEROPLANE.

"Men, I have an announcement to make," said Lieutenant De Frees, when they had all assembled with their various types of machines. Ned noticed that the officer held in his hand a sheet of blue paper of official appearance. It was closely covered with typewritten matter.

"Py golly, vot now comes?" whispered Hans to Mulligan.

"Whist, can't ye, and listen to the officer!" warned Mulligan.

Like the rest, the two whisperers fell into attitudes of deep attention.

"As you all are aware," began the officer, "it is the purpose of the navy to determine the advisability of equipping every vessel in the fleet with an aeroplane suitable for bomb dropping or scout duty. Naturally one of the most essential features of such a craft would be its ability to fly both to and from the parent ship. In other words, not only must it be able to fly from the ship to the shore, a comparatively simple matter, but it must be able to land back on the deck of the ship from whence it came—a far more hazardous feat."

"Vos is idt, dot 'haz-az-abluss'?" whispered Hans.

"You all follow my meaning?" asked the officer.

A chorus of "Aye, aye, sir," came from the throats of the "Aviation Class."

"Py Chimmy Hill, I follow you all righd, budt I'm a long, long vay behindt, as der terrapin remarked to der rappit," commented Hans in a low undertone which was lost in the hearty roar of the concerted response.

"Very good," resumed the officer. "Now, then, I have here," he referred to the sheet of typewritten paper, "an announcement from the department that one week hence a landing platform

ON AERO SERVICE 75

will be erected on the after-deck of the *Manhattan*. She will anchor in the Roads, and those desiring to attempt the feat of landing on her deck may notify me at the earliest opportunity. I may add, that to the successful aviator, will accrue an award of $100, beside certain promotion for efficiency."

"Nodt for vun million billion bundtles of dollars vould I preak my neck," commented Hans to Mulligan.

"By gorry, Dutchy, I don't blame ye. 'Twould be a day's wu-urk fer a burrd to do the thrick," was the response.

"We will now take up morning practice," came the next announcement. "I think that some of you are far enough advanced to try passenger carrying across country. Strong, I assign you to take up Taylor. Merritt, you will carry Chance as your companion."

A sort of buzz of excitement ran through the squad, as the chosen ones hurried off to make ready.

"The remainder of the squad," came the next order, "will resume ordinary practice."

"Dot's all ve do, is resuming," muttered Hans. "I hope I don't resume my sneezing, py crickety."

It did not take Ned and Herc long to get ready. With a buzz and whirr, they were up and into the air before Merritt and Chance got their engines tuned up. No directions as to the course they should take had been given them, so Ned headed the flying machine off inland, where fields and hedges showed in a pretty patchwork beneath them, with a rim of blue mountains in the distance.

"Say, this is great," exclaimed Herc, as they sped on,—

"Take a trip up to the sky;
Say, but it's a dream to fly;
From the ground we'll take a jump,
I hope we don't land with a bump."

"You're improving as a poet every minute," laughed Ned, his alert eyes peering straight ahead and his hands firmly grasping the controlling wheel. "Let's hope you're not a prophet as well as a poet. By the way, just take a look round and see if you can catch a glimpse of those other two fellows."

"I see them, about ten miles behind," announced Herc presently. "They're coming right ahead, too. Traveling at a faster clip than we are, I judge."

"Let them risk their necks if they want to. We'll jog along easily," replied Ned.

For some time they sped on, above pastures and grain fields, and patches of woodland and meadow, threaded here and there by narrow streams which glittered in the bright sunlight like silver ribbons. It was, as Herc had said, "great." The blood ran faster, and every nerve tingled invigoratingly under the stimulus of the rapid advance through the air. All about them the shining stay-wires hummed and buzzed, giving out a shrill accompaniment to the steady drone of the motor.

"I'll slow down a bit now," said Ned presently.

"I'm anxious to see how she'll behave at reduced speed with extra weight on board."

As he shut down the power, the aeroplane descended perceptibly. The added weight of another passenger made her far less buoyant, as was to have been expected.

They were quite low, hovering like a big hawk above a small farm-house, when a sudden scream from below was borne to their ears quite distinctly.

"Hullo! What's that?" exclaimed Ned.

"It was a woman screaming," was the rejoinder. "We'd better drop down and see what's the trouble."

"Just what I think. It came from that farm-house."

"I know. Hold on tight, now; I'm going to drop fast."

Like a stone the aeroplane fell. The rapidity of the drop made both the aviators gasp. Just as it seemed inevitable that they must be dashed to bits on the ground beneath, Ned, by a skilful bit of airmanship, brought his craft to a level keel, and alighted without a jolt.

They came to earth in an open meadow at the rear of the farm-house, a white-painted, green-shuttered place of comfortable appearance. As the machine stopped its motion, both lads leaped out and began running toward the house. As they neared it, a voice struck on their ears:

"Come on, now; no nonsense. Give me the money your husband has hidden here, or I'll hurt you."

Had the two Dreadnought Boys been able to see through the walls of the house, they would have beheld a terrified woman, in a gingham gown and white apron, cowering before a heavy-set man, who was brandishing a stout club. The fellow's look was desperate. His deep little eyes glittered menacingly under heavy, black brows. His bluish, bristly chin thrust forward truculently.

"Take these silver spoons," the woman begged, "and leave me alone. They are all I have."

"Don't try lying to me," growled the man, stepping forward a pace. "It won't go. I've heard around here that your husband is a miser, and I want the money he has hidden. Come, now, are you going to give it to me, or——"

He raised the club threateningly.

The woman paled, but stood her ground bravely.

"I have given you all the valuables we have in the house," she said. "If anyone told you my husband was a miser, they must have done it out of malice. We are poor farmers, and——"

"That'll do! That'll do! I'm tired of argying with yer. I'll look for myself. Stand aside, and look jumpy now, or——"

A scream burst from the woman's lips, as her brutal annoyer came toward her, his upper lip curled in a snarl.

But he had not advanced more than a couple of paces before an unexpected interruption occurred. A third voice struck into the scene.

"Stop right where you are, Bill Kennell, or there'll be trouble."

Kennell, for it was the disgraced and desperate bully formerly of the *Manhattan,* whipped round in a flash. His recognition of the Dreadnought Boys, who stood in the opened kitchen door, was swift as theirs had been of him.

"Ned Strong!" he exclaimed in a husky voice.

"Not forgetting Herc Taylor, Bill," grinned the freckle-faced youth. "You don't seem exactly glad to see us."

"Oh, whoever you are, thank heaven you have come!" cried the woman. She reeled backward, overcome by the reaction of her feelings, and would have fallen if Herc had not jumped forward and seized her in his arms.

At the same instant, Kennell, who had lost none of his former agility, crouched and sprung like a wildcat at Ned. But if he had thought to catch the Dreadnought Boy off his guard, he was dreadfully mistaken. Ned jumped nimbly to one side, as Kennell rushed at him, and the bully carried by the impetus of his onrush, crashed against the wall. He recovered himself in an instant and came back at Ned with formidable force. But once more Ned was ready for him. The Dreadnought Boy dived suddenly, as Kennell raised his knotted club, and, coming up under the man's arm, caught him a blow on the chin that caused the former bully of the *Manhattan* to reel and stagger.

But, as if he had been prepared for some such result of his onslaught, Kennell, without an instant's loss of time, produced a pistol from somewhere amid his tattered garments.

Before Ned could make another move, a hot flame fanned his face; a loud report rang in his ears, and he felt a sharp, stinging pain in his head. Then he lost consciousness.

As he fell with a crash against a chair, bringing it a splintered wreck to the floor with him, Herc deposited the fainting woman on an old-fashioned settee, and sprang with a roar of anger at Kennell. But as he did so, two other figures suddenly appeared in the open doorway of the farm-house kitchen.

"It's Bill Kennell!" cried one of them, who was no other than Merritt. He and Chance had seen Ned's descent, and had dropped, too, to see if, perchance, some bad luck had not overtaken their rivals. Hearing the uproar in the kitchen, they had hastened to it.

As Herc fairly leaped on Kennell, before the ruffian had a chance to fire another shot, Merritt took in the whole situation with the quick intuition of a man of his intellect.

Kennell, with Herc on the top of him, was tottering backward, and on the verge of falling helplessly before his powerful young antagonist, when Merritt, with a quick movement, picked up a heavy chair. Raising it, he brought it down with all his might on the unconscious Herc's head. The next instant the two Dreadnought Boys lay senseless on the floor of the kitchen, one of them seemingly badly wounded.

CHAPTER VIII.

HERC GETS "A TALKING TO."

When Ned came to himself, it was to find the farmer's wife bending over him and laving the wound on his head with warm water. Herc, with a quizzical look on his face, stood nearby.

"Whoof!" he exclaimed, as Ned opened his eyes. "What struck us?"

"I guess a bullet nicked me," grinned Ned; "it isn't much of a wound, is it?"

"Only grazed the skin," the farmer's wife assured him. "I am so thankful. It would have been terrible if either of you had come to serious harm through your brave act in my defence."

"Oh, that's all right, ma'am," said Ned, scrambling to his feet, "glad to have been of service. But whatever hit you, Herc?"

For Herc was holding his head now, with a lugubrious expression.

"Blessed if I know. Wish I did. I saw you fall, and jumped in to land Kennell. I grabbed him, and was bearing him down, when something that felt like a locomotive hit me a fearful wallop. Then I went to slumberland."

"Oh, how frightened I was, when I recovered my senses, and saw you two brave lads lying on the floor," said the farmer's wife, almost overcome at the recollection.

"Well, unless this house is haunted by spooks, who can hit as hard as steam-hammers, we'll have to come to the conclusion that Kennell had some confederates," decided Herc.

"The whole thing has a queer look to me," admitted Ned, with a puzzled look. "I can't make it out at all. You are sure that the fellow who annoyed you had no companions, madam?"

"I'm certain," declared the farmer's wife positively. "He came here soon after my husband drove off to town. He asked for something to eat, which I gave him. When he had finished he frightened me by demanding money. I gave him what little I had, but he insisted that my husband had more concealed about the premises. If you had not come in time, I do not know what I should have done. But whom have I got to thank? You—you," looking hesitatingly at the queer combination of aviation costume and regulation jackie uniform the lads wore, "you aren't soldiers, be you?"

"Not yet, ma'am," rejoined Herc gravely, "although at times we are tempted to soldier."

"We're soldiers' first cousins," laughed Ned.

"Oh, I see, sailors. But then, what is that contraption out there?" She pointed out of the window at the aeroplane. "I saw one like it at the county fair. Be you flying sailors?"

"I guess that's just what we are, ma'am?" laughed Ned. "And that reminds me that we must be getting along. It is going on for noon."

He appeared about to go, and Herc was following his example, when the woman checked them.

"Oh, you must not go till you have told me

your names," she said. "My husband would like to thank you personally for your bravery."

"As for our names, they are soon given," said Ned. "But for thanks—I guess it's the duty of Uncle Sam's sailors to do all they can to help the weak, and——"

"Land the bullies," finished Herc, with a flourish of his fist.

"Only this time it looks as if the bully had landed us," put in Ned, with a chuckle.

"Humph!" grunted Herc, feeling his head ruefully. "But," he added, cheering up vastly, "we had him on the run, anyhow."

"That's so," agreed Ned, "and I see, 'by the same token,' as Mulligan says, that he was in such a hurry he left the spoons behind him."

He pointed to a scattered heap at the door which the farmer's wife pounced upon gratefully. The spoons were all there but one, and Kennell's exit must have been hurried, to judge by this fact. Evidently he had dropped them by accident and had not tarried to pick them up.

While the farmer's wife looked on in wonderment, and not a little fear, Ned and Herc prepared their machine for flight. In a little less than ten minutes' time, they had taken the air with a roar and whirr, throwing the domestic animals about the place into panic. Without incident they winged their way back to the aviation field, arriving there in time for a hearty noonday dinner at the farmhouse.

Ned's head was bandaged, and Herc's cheek was swollen, but they volunteered no explanation of their injuries, and Lieutenant De Frees concluded that they had met with some slight accident of which they did not care to speak, and deemed it best not to ask questions.

During the noon-day meal, Ned watched the countenances of Merritt and Chance narrowly. Although he had not the slightest thing to base his belief upon, an obstinate idea had entered his head and would not leave it, and that was, that they had, in some manner, something to do with the occurrences of the morning. He mentioned this to Herc afterward, but was laughed at for his pains.

"It was some sort of a hard-hitting ghost that landed me that sleep wallop," declared Herc, who, as we know, was reprehensibly given to slang on all occasions.

The afternoon passed quietly. Merritt and Chance asked leave to go into the town, which was not far off, and they were granted an afternoon's furlough. In what manner they employed it, we shall learn before long. Ned and Herc watched them go off, arm in arm, and Herc turned to Ned with an indignant snort.

"Whoof! I'll bet those chaps are up to some more cussedness. Look how they've got their heads together. Wonder what they are plotting now?"

"Don't know, and don't much care," laughed Ned; "tell you what, Herc, you'd better get out and practice, instead of wasting time on speculations over Merritt, Chance and Co. By the way, I wonder what they would say if they knew that their old acquaintance, Kennell, was at large and up to his old tricks?"

"Join him, probably. Especially if it was in anything that would make trouble for us," returned Herc. "But what are you going to do this afternoon?"

Herc had noticed that Ned had not donned his aviation "uniform."

"I? Oh, Lieutenant De Frees told me I could get my drawings in shape for his examination of them to-night. He is to have one or two naval experts at his quarters, whom he is anxious to show them to. Herc, old boy, maybe we're on the highway to fame."

"Maybe you are, you mean," flashed back Herc. "I guess I'll be the same old stick-in-the-mud till the end of the chapter."

"Nonsense. Use your initiative. Think up something new in connection with our present line of work."

"A new way to tumble, for instance," grinned Herc.

"There you go. That's your great fault. You can never be serious for two minutes together."

"I can, too," remonstrated Herc indignantly. "That time I was in the brig on the *Manhattan* I was serious till—till they brought my dinner."

Ned couldn't help laughing at his whimsical chum's frank way of putting things. But presently he resumed, more seriously.

"Come, Herc, you don't do yourself justice. You laugh away your real ability. Look here, I'll give you an idea to work on. See what you can do with it."

"I'm all cheers—ears, I mean," declared Herc, leaning forward in interested fashion.

Ned realized that the flippant tone hid real interest. Without seeming to notice it, he went on.

"One of the most needed improvements in the modern aeroplane—I mean where it is used in warfare—is a perfected appliance for bomb-dropping. The present way is pretty clumsy. An aviator has to let go of his controls with one hand while he manipulates his bomb-dropping device with the other. Some bit of apparatus that would do the work, say by foot-power, would be a big improvement, and add a whole lot to the effectiveness of the machine using it."

Herc kindled to enthusiasm while Ned talked. His careless manner vanished.

"That's like you, Ned," he said with real warmth of affection, "always ready to help a fellow out. I'll try to work out something on the lines you suggested. It's time I did something, anyhow. But the idea will still be yours, no matter what I do with it."

"Pshaw!" chuckled Ned, "didn't Shakespeare work over old stories into great plays?"

"I suppose so," agreed Herc, who did not care to display his almost total darkness concerning the late Mr. Shakespeare and his methods.

CHAPTER IX.

A CONSPIRACY IS RIPENING.

"That you, boys?"

The speaker emerged from a patch of gloomy looking bushes, masking an old stone bridge.

"Yes, it's us all right, Herr Muller. On time, ain't we?"

It was Chance who spoke. Close behind came Merritt and another figure.

"Yes, you're on time, all right. But who's that with you? I don't want outsiders mixed up in this."

Merritt came forward with the third member of the newly arrived party. "This is Bill Kennell, an old chum of ours," he said. "He's all right, and we may find him useful in our plans."

"Very well, if you'll vouch for him."

It was noticeable that all trace of accent had now vanished from Herr Muller's tone. In fact, except for a very slight trace of foreign pronunciation, impossible to reproduce, he spoke remarkably good English.

"Oh, we'll vouch for him. And now to business," said Merritt, seating himself on the coping of the bridge. "You said this afternoon that you, as representative of the New York group of International Anarchists, would pay us well to keep you in possession of the latest moves of the United States navy."

"Yes, yes," responded the other eagerly, "we wish to know all—everything—I am authorized to pay you well for such information."

"But why—why do you want it?" demanded Chance bluntly.

"I will tell you. We anarchists hate all law and order. We wish to be a law to ourselves. All law is oppression. Such is our teaching. Navies and armies represent power and help to keep law and order, therefore, when the time comes, we wish"—he paused reflectively—"to destroy all such tools of oppression."

Chance, calloused as he was, gasped.

ON AERO SERVICE

"You mean you would dare to destroy or try to damage, the property of the United States?" he gasped.

"I mean what I said, my young man."

"Oh, say, count us out, then. That's too much for me. Say, Merritt, let's be getting back."

"Hold on a minute," snarled the masquerading photographer, changing in an instant from a docile creature into an alert, dangerous martinet, "you can't refuse to fall in with my plans now. If you do I shall crush you. You are in my power now."

"Pooh!" scoffed Merritt. "How do you make that out?"

But, though he strove to make his tone easy, there was an under note of anxiety in it.

"How do I make it out? In this way, my friends: If you are false to your promises to me, I shall denounce you to the government authorities. I have witnesses to all that you said this afternoon in my room at the hotel. The man you thought was a waiter was in my employ, and is an anarchist, like myself. That shabby little peddler who came to sell some cheap jewelry was another of the same belief. They heard all you said. Moreover, they saw you accept money from me——"

"But you told us that all you wanted us to do was to get those plans from Ned Strong when he comes along this way from the lieutenant's house to-night," gasped Chance.

"Yes; but I may have other uses for you. Rest assured that you are in a web from which you cannot escape. If you try to play false to me, I will have you sent to the place which Uncle Sam reserves for traitors and spies."

"Oh, well," said Merritt slyly, "we may as well make the best of it. Let's talk business. In the first place, did you bring the disguises?"

Herr Muller, as we must know him, rejoined in the affirmative. "I have them in that old barn," he said.

"Very well. The time is getting along. We had better go up there and assume them. By the way, have you any pistols for us? We couldn't smuggle out our service revolvers."

"Pistols!" scoffed the other. "What do you want pistols for? Are there not three of you against one? And I will be in reserve in case he proves too much for you."

"Um, I know; that's all very well," muttered Chance, "but you don't know this fellow Strong. He's as powerful as a bull, and will fight like a wild-cat."

"But he's up against overpowering odds tonight," Merritt rejoined, with regained confidence. "This is the time that Ned Strong, the favored paragon of the navy, is going to get his —and get it good."

"You can bet he is," agreed Chance and Kennell, with clenched teeth.

"I've got a few scores to pay off on my own account," added the latter.

"Well, here are your disguises," said Herr Muller, striking a match and indicating a bundle in one corner of the barn. Presently he produced a pocket flash-lamp, and held it cautiously while Merritt and Chance, two traitors to the United States, invested themselves in the rough-looking garments he had provided. They were complete, even to false whiskers. When they had attired themselves in the tattered clothes and adjusted the remainder of their disguises, two more disreputable-looking specimens of the genus tramp than Merritt and Chance presented could not have been imagined.

"You'll do finely," declared Herr Muller, with deep satisfaction, when the preparations were concluded. "I'd be scared of you myself, if I met you on a dark road," he added, with peculiar humor.

"How about me?" asked Kennell. "That 'Dreadnought Boy,' as they call him, knows me."

"Pshaw! that's so," said Herr Muller. "Well, see here," producing a handkerchief, "tie this over the lower part of your face and you will be well enough disguised."

"I reckon so," agreed Kennell, adopting the suggestion.

In the meantime, Ned had been practically the guest of honor at Lieutenant De Free's quarters. Two or three other naval officers were present, and they all displayed frank interest in the bright, intelligent youth and his invention, which he explained at length.

"But, my dear De Frees," one of them—a young ensign named Tandy—had declared, "you can say all you like about the aeroplane in warfare. In efficiency it will never take the place of the submarine, for instance. I'm willing to wager any amount that on any night that I held the deck, an aeroplane, equipped with pontoons or anything else, could not, by any possibility, approach within a hundred yards of my vessel."

"You really think so, Tandy?" queried Lieutenant De Frees good-naturedly. "Well, I tell you what we will do: At some other time we'll meet and talk it over. If you are still in the same mind, we will draw up conditions for such a test. It should be interesting and of great value theoretically."

"Yes," laughed Tandy, "it will demonstrate the fact that no aerial craft could torpedo or blow up a war vessel at night without being perceived in time. Therefore, what is the use of equipping the ships with such craft? They take up valuable room and waste a lot of money which would be better spent on guns and ordnance."

"I agree with you, Tandy," said Lieutenant Morrow, a veteran of many years' service, "from my observation of aeroplanes, one could not get within bomb-dropping or torpedo-aiming distance of a war vessel at night. Why, the noise of their engines would alone betray their nearness."

"But what if she glided up on pontoons?" smiled Lieutenant De Frees.

"The same thing would hold good," declared young Ensign Tandy, with a confident air.

Of course, Ned, as a petty officer, could not

take part in this conversation, but it made a deep impression on him. After warm goodnights from the officers, who really felt an admiration for this clean-cut and self-respecting, although perfectly respectful young sailor, Ned set out on his homeward way. In his breast-pocket—or rather tucked inside his loose blouse—he carried the plans of his invention.

It was quite dark, with the exception of a pallid light given out by a sickly moon, that was every now and then obscured altogether by hurrying clouds. Ned walked along quickly, at his usual swinging pace. His thoughts were too much upon his invention for him to pay much attention to his surroundings.

All at once, however, he stopped short and listened for an instant. But not a sound, except the sighing of a light, night wind in the trees that bordered the road, disturbed the stillness.

"Funny," mused Ned; "I could have been certain I saw a light flash by that old bridge right ahead. I guess I'm seeing things, too, like Herc."

So thinking, he struck once more into his regular pace. A few steps brought him into a patch of velvety shadow caused by the thick-growing shrubs and alders that edged the creek which the bridge spanned.

"What a spot for a hold-up!" thought the young man-o'-war's-man, when he entered the blackness. As he did so, a sharp chill struck him. A keen sense of impending danger caused him to swing sharply around.

It was well he had heeded his intuition, for, as he turned, a heavy bludgeon whistled by his ear. It had been aimed for his head, but his sudden and unexpected move had saved him.

For a breath, Ned stood rooted to the spot. Then his eyes blazed with anger.

"Come on, you skulking thieves!" he cried in a high, clear voice, "I'm ready for you!"

CHAPTER X.

A DREADNOUGHT BOY AT BAY.

The Dreadnought Boy's challenge was still vibrating when, from every side, dark figures seemed to spring. They rushed at him like so many tigers. Ned struck out blindly.

It was hard to distinguish anything in the darkness, but twice in the first few seconds of his desperate battle against odds, he felt his fists encounter some one's features. The feeling gave him a sense of distinct satisfaction.

"One! Two!" counted the young man-o'-war's-man grimly, as his fists shot out right and left like sledge-hammers.

But Ned knew, as well as his opponents, that four to one are almost insurmountable odds. Already he had knocked two of his foes sprawling, when he was struck a blow from behind that staggered him. But it was only for an instant.

The next moment he had turned and seized by the throat the man who had aimed the blow. He shook him as a terrier shakes a rat. He could hear the fellow's teeth chatter, but it was too dark to distinguish features.

In the meantime, his fallen opponents had picked themselves up. So far the fight had progressed in ominous silence, save for the deep breaths and stamping feet of those engaged in it. But now, fury at this unexpectedly stubborn resistance brought words to the lips of his foes. They were not nice words, and Ned thrilled with a desire to silence their utterers, for he was a clean-spoken boy, who hated profanity in any form.

Suddenly, as if by concerted consent, his foes ceased their separate attacks, and massed like a wolf pack preparing to finish its prey. Ned had hardly sensed the new situation and braced himself to meet it before they were upon him.

Thud! thud!

The lad's fists met their mark fairly, and once

more two of his opponents reeled back. But this time they did not fall. Instead, they rallied to the attack.

As if they had been one, all four of his assailants hurled themselves on the Dreadnought Boy. Strive as he would, Ned felt his arms pinioned to his sides, and he was borne down by sheer weight of numbers. He struggled with every steel-like muscle in his powerful young body. With teeth set and eyes that flamed, he fought with every fraction of an ounce of strength he possessed. But, with two men hanging like bulldogs to his neck from behind, and two more clinging to his arms and battering him in front, the lad could do nothing. With a sickening sense of helplessness, he felt a leg slide under his, and tottered backward.

With his four foes still clinging like leeches to him, Ned felt himself borne to earth, and then, despite his frantic struggles, a hand was thrust rapidly into each of his pockets. A cry escaped him for the first time—a cry of rage.

The rascals were rifling him of the plans of the pontoon-equipped aeroplane!

All at once a voice struck into the scene. Some one was coming down the road. At the top of a pair of lusty lungs the approaching individual was singing:

"A sailor's wife, a sail-or's star should be!
Star-r-r-r-r-r should be!
Star-r-r-r-r-r should be!"

"Herc!" shouted Ned.

"Ahoy, there!" came the hearty response, as Herc, who had been sauntering along the road, on his way to meet Ned, broke into a run. Something in the accent of Ned's cry had warned him that his comrade's need for help was urgent.

"Scatter!" came a sharp voice from one of the hitherto silent waylayers of the Dreadnought Boy.

Like so many leaves before a sharp puff of autumn wind, they instantly dissolved into the night. Ned, dusty, battered and furious, picked himself up. As he did so Herc plunged into the dark patch in which the desperate fight had taken place. He hailed Ned and received an instant response.

"What on earth has happened?" he exclaimed.

Ned soon told his story. His voice throbbed with anger as he talked. Ned was slow to wrath, but once aroused he was whole-souled in his anger, and surely he had justification for his rage.

"The scoundrels!" burst out Herc, "couldn't you recognize any of them?"

"No. They chose the place well. I could hardly tell you if it wasn't for your voice."

"I'll bet the hole out of a doughnut that Merritt and Chance had something to do with this."

"I don't know. I hardly know anything I'm so mad. At any rate I must have marked one or two of them. My knuckles are skinned where I hit them."

"Let's hope that Merritt and Chance were the

two you walloped. If so, we shan't have much difficulty in identifying two of your assailants."

"You talk as if you were certain they had something to do with it."

"I am," responded Herc briefly.

"Tell you what we'll do," said Ned, suddenly, "let's light a match and look the ground over. Maybe we can find some trace of the fellows' identity. There's one thing sure, they were not common robbers."

"That's evident enough. It was the plans they were after. But who that knows about them could use them to advantage?"

"That remains to be seen. In the meantime, on second thoughts, I can do better than matches. I've got that small electric torch I use about the aeroplane."

"Good. Switch it on and we'll see what we can see."

Ned drew out a small object from his pocket. There was a sharp click and a bright ray of light shot out. Here and there about the ground the Dreadnought Boy flashed the tiny searchlight.

"Look here!" cried Herc suddenly.

In triumph he held up a tangled looking object.

"What is it?" asked Ned in a puzzled tone.

"That's easy. It's false hair like the kind we used on the *Manhattan* when we gave that show. The chaps that attacked you were disguised and this was a part of their makeup."

"I think so, too. But—shades of immortal Farragut!—look here, Herc!" Ned, as he spoke, pounced on a roll of papers lying in the dust at one side of the road, right under a clump of alder bushes.

"It's the plans!" gasped Herc.

"That's right," rejoined Ned, opening the roll and glancing at its contents, "they're all intact, too. One of the rascals that took them must have placed them in his pocket. Then, in pushing into this brush to escape, they were caught and thrown out."

"I guess that's it, and a good thing for us, too. But—gee whiz!"

Without another word Herc plunged into the brush. He fought his way through it furiously. Happening to look up while they had been talking he had caught the glint of a pair of eyes as the light from Ned's torch reflected in them. One of the men had noted the loss of the plans and had returned for them. That much was evident. At any rate, Herc, as usual, acted before he thought, and in two bounds was swallowed in the brush.

Ned, not realizing in the least what had happened, and half inclined to think that Herc had gone suddenly crazy, followed instantly. Presently he found himself at Herc's side. The freckle-faced lad gasped out a few disconnected sentences. Broken as they were, they apprised Ned of what had happened.

"The rascal must have come back to get the plans," he concluded; "I suppose he was watching us and waiting his chance to emerge into the road when the light glinted on his eyeballs."

"Oh, if we could only have captured him!"

"More especially," put in Herc dryly, "as I recognized the man as Chance."

"What! You did!"

"Sure. I could swear to it. This is the time they've overreached themselves. They tried to steal the plans for some reason best known to themselves, and failed. They tried to disguise their part in the job and failed. I guess their career in the navy has ended for good and all now. In the morning we——"

A pair of arms were thrown round Herc's neck from behind. Caught all unprepared, he was carried off his feet in a flash and in a second a stout cord had been whipped about his wrists confining his hands helplessly behind his back. While this had been going on Ned was served the same trick.

In a trice the two Dreadnought Boys were rendered helpless, where an instant before Herc had been crowing over their triumph.

Somebody aimed a vicious kick at Ned's face which he dodged by rolling over on his side. At the same time a spiteful voice snarled:

"Our career has ended, eh? Well, it looks to me more as if you were rapidly approaching your own finish."

The voice was that of Chance, and his chuckle of triumph was echoed by his three companions who stood about the recumbent boys, rejoicing in the bit of strategy which had wrought their undoing.

CHAPTER XI.

IN THEIR ENEMIES' HANDS.

"Well," said Ned, in the calm, even tone which seemed to come to him in all emergencies, "what do you mean to do with us now?"

"Yah!" jeered Chance, thrusting his face forward evilly, "you think we'll tell you, don't yer? You just lie there and don't get up if you know what's good for you."

As he spoke he produced a pistol as if to emphasize his warning.

"You can't scare us in that way, Chance," resumed Ned, "you wouldn't dare to——"

"You don't know what I'd dare," retorted Chance; "I hate you, Ned Strong, and now it's my chance to get even with you and with your butting-in chum."

"Come, don't talk any more nonsense," rejoined Ned, "I can make allowances for a small nature actuated by motives of meanness and jealousy. But it's about time to end this nonsense. We'll be late for lights out if we don't all get back. If you'll come to your proper minds and end this foolishness, I'll promise not to report anything about to-night's work, unless questions are asked, and then I'll have to tell the truth."

Merritt had been talking apart with the two others, whom we know were Herr Muller and Bill Kennell, but whose identity was, of course, a mystery to the boys. He now came forward. He was just in time to catch Ned's last words.

"Maybe you won't get a chance to tell the truth or anything else, Ned Strong," he said; "as for injuring us with the navy, you couldn't do that if you tried. We're through with it."

"You're going to desert?" demanded Ned.

"Just what I'd have expected of you two rats," snorted Herc.

"Call it deserting, if you like," parried Merritt, "I call it quitting just as——"

ON AERO SERVICE 115

"Oh, you're a quitter all right," struck in Herc, "a quitter from Quitterville—one of the first settlers there, I guess."

"Are you going to be quiet?" hissed Chance.

"When I get good and ready, as the thunderstorm said to the old maid who complained she couldn't sleep," responded the freckle-faced lad.

"Leave him alone," said Merritt, "we can afford to let them talk their heads off if they want to; they'll be quiet enough before long."

"Well, come on. Let us be moving," interpolated Herr Muller's voice; "himmel! we have a long tramp before us."

"That's right," assented Merritt, then, turning to Chance, he went on in a low tone, "It was a good thing that we decided on that place this afternoon. It's not more than three miles from here. We can get there, put these two cubs under lock and key, and be snug in bed without giving the alarm, if we're cautious."

Chance nodded and gave his unpleasant chuckle.

"Has Muller got the keys?" he asked.

"Yes. On the plea that we wanted to explore the place the old watchman, who hasn't been near it for a month, loaned them to him."

Ned caught some of this conversation and his heart sank. It appeared plain enough that their rascally captors had already decided on a place to confine them. Some isolated building, so he judged, though what its nature could be he could not imagine.

"Come, get up," snarled Chance, addressing the lads as soon as his colloquy with Merritt was concluded.

"We will when you take these bracelets off our ankles," rejoined Herc, motioning with his head at the ropes which bound their feet.

Merritt and Chance quickly cut loose the Dreadnought Boys' foot thongs and Ned and Herc stood erect. But if they had entertained any idea of escape, it was quickly cut short.

"See this," warned Chance, tapping a pistol which belonged to Kennell. "It's got a silencer on it, and if either of you try to run you'll get a dose of lead, and, as the report isn't louder than an air rifle, nobody will be the wiser."

Ned nodded.

"I compliment you on your generalship," he said contemptuously.

A few seconds later they moved off. Muller led the way. By his side shuffled a figure strangely familiar to both lads, but neither of them could place it. All their efforts to catch a glimpse of the two leaders' features were cheated too, both by the light and the fact that they kept their faces studiously turned away.

They pressed on for a mile or two through woods and across fields, and presently a whiff of salt-laden air struck Ned in the face.

"We're getting near the sea," he thought. "I wonder if they mean to take us off some place in a boat?"

But conversation had now ceased between Chance and Merritt, and the others were too far ahead for the lads to catch a word. Before long they emerged, without warning, from a clump of woods, directly upon a wide expanse of salt meadows. The lonely wastes stretched as far as the eye could see. Fleeting glimpses of moonlight, as the clouds swept across the sky, showed the glimmer of the ocean beyond. They could catch the sullen roar of the surf on the beach.

Without hesitation, Herr Muller struck out across the salt meadows, following a narrow path between the hummocks of salt grass. Here and there they crossed stretches of marshy land where the oozy mud came to their ankles.

All at once there suddenly shot up from the gloomy wastes the rectangular outlines of a large building of some kind. As they drew closer to the dark bulk the boys could see that the walls were pierced with numerous windows in monotonous rows. Soon the further fact became evident that each window was barred. There was something indescribably depressing about the aspect,—the gloomy, vast outlines of the dark, de-

ON AERO SERVICE

serted building ahead of them, and the pallidly moonlit wastes of salt meadow all about it.

What could the place be? No light appeared in any of the numerous apertures, and the silence hung heavily about it. Suddenly there flashed across Ned the recollection of a flight he had taken some days before when he had soared above a building which, in the daylight, resembled this lonely place. The sight of it standing isolated and vast in the midst of its wild surroundings had impressed him, and on his return he had inquired about it. They had told him that it was an old lunatic asylum. The state had erected it there some years before, but the atmosphere of the salt meadows had proved malarious, and it had been abandoned.

A bulbous-nosed, red-faced old tippler in the village had also been pointed out to him as a man who held down "a soft snap," by being appointed "watchman" to the deserted pile. Evidently the keys had been obtained from him and the gloomy buildings were their destination.

That this was the case they were speedily to learn. Herr Muller approached a stout-looking door, in the top of which was a small, grated opening. Inserting a key he turned the lock and flung the door open. A damp, decaying odor,—the breath of a deserted human dwelling place,—rushed out. In spite of himself Ned shuddered. It reminded him of the crypt of an old church he had inspected in Spain when the ships were on their European cruise.

Muller, who seemed to know the way, threaded several long passages carrying a candle which he had ignited at the doorway. In this manner they traversed a considerable distance. At every turn fresh corridors, long and empty, appeared. The place was a maze of passages and stairways.

At length he paused in front of a rather small door at the end of a hall which, judging from the stairs they had climbed, must have been near the top of the building. He flung this door open, and the next instant the candle was extinguished,—evidently with the intention of concealing his features,—and the boys were roughly thrust forward.

If they had not been taken totally by surprise they might have resisted. But the shoves came suddenly, and projected them into a room through the door before they realized what was happening. The next instant the door clanged behind them, just as Herc hurled himself against it.

They heard the lock grate and some bolts clang heavily as they were fastened in.

"Bottled!" gasped Herc, truthfully if slangily.

But Ned had pulled out his pocket lantern and was examining the place in which they had been imprisoned. He was struck by something peculiar about it. He reached out a hand and felt the walls. They were smooth and yielding. They had been covered with some soft substance. High up was a small window with thick metal bars.

"What sort of a place is this?" gasped Herc as he, in his turn, felt the yielding, cushioned walls. "These walls feel like the upholstered chairs in the skipper's cabin."

Ned battled with a catch in his voice before he replied. He had grasped the truth of their almost hopeless situation.

"Herc, old boy," he said, putting a hand on his shipmate's shoulder, "brace up for a shock. This place is a deserted lunatic asylum, and they've locked us in what was formerly used as a padded cell for solitary confinement."

CHAPTER XII.

"STOP WHERE YOU ARE!"

It is a curious fact that most absolutely overwhelming predicaments do not at first strike in upon their victims with the crushing force that would be imagined. This was evidenced by Herc's rejoinder to Ned's startling information.

"Great ginger!" he exclaimed, "I guess we're in just the place where we belong. If we hadn't gone blundering into that trap we wouldn't have been in this fix, and if we hadn't——"

"Left the farm and enlisted in the navy we wouldn't have been here either," retorted Ned.

A scrutiny of their prison confirmed Ned in his first judgment of its character. The walls, though padded, were solid, and seemingly impenetrable. The window was far too high up to be reached, and even if they could have got to it, it could be seen that the steel bars were set solidly into the masonry. The door, which was examined in its turn, proved to be likewise of solid oak. No lock appeared on it. Doubtless this was to prevent any of the unfortunates formerly confined in the place from injuring themselves on projecting bolts.

At the bottom of the door, however, a peculiar contrivance appeared. It was a small, hinged flap, which, when raised, revealed an opening some six inches square. The thought suggested itself to Ned that it might have been used once as a means for giving food or drink to the incurables confined within during their violent spells.

He opened the flap and thrust his hand through. A vague hope had entered his mind that he might be able to reach up as far as the bolts on the outside. If he could have done this he could have opened them. But, as might have been expected, this was not feasible. Ned had the exasperating experience of being able, by the utmost exertion, to touch the bottom of the bolt with his finger-tips, but that was all. Even then he had to shove his arm so far through the hole that it was grazed and sore when he withdrew it.

"W-e-l-l?" said Herc slowly, as they sank down side by side on a sort of bench, padded like the rest of the interior of the place.

"W-e-l-l?" retorted Ned, "so far as I can see, if we were sealed up in one of the *Manhattan's* air-tight magazines we would have just about as good a chance of getting out as we have of escaping from this place."

"Same here," agreed Herc woefully. "What are we going to do? Do you think they'll starve us to death?"

Barren of hope as the situation appeared, Ned could not help smiling at Herc's woebegone tone.

"They'd hardly dare to do that," he rejoined; "this is the twentieth century, and such things as law and order prevail. No, I guess they have some sort of trickery on hand with which we might interfere, and they mean to keep us locked up here till they have carried out their rascally plans."

"Talking of plans, did they take back the ones of the pontoon aeroplane?"

"No," exclaimed Ned, brightening, "thank goodness that's one thing they seem to have forgotten. Anyhow I suppose they know they have us at their mercy and can get them any time they want them."

"Reckon that's it," agreed Herc.

Silence ensued. The two boys sat side by side in the pitchy blackness of their prison, for Ned, anxious to reserve it for emergencies, had extinguished the electric torch. Neither of them was a nervous sort of youth, but the long vigil in the dark was enough to get on anybody's nerves.

"This is certainly a tough situation," remarked Ned after a time. He spoke more for the sake of hearing his own voice than for any novel idea the words might convey.

"Not giving up, are you, Ned?" inquired Herc.

"Giving up?" grated out the elder Dreadnought Boy, "I'm like Paul Jones—I've just begun to fight."

"When did Paul Jones say that?" asked Herc.

"Why, that time that the British captain, Pearson, peered through the smoke surrounding his majesty's ship *Serapis* and the little *Bonhomme Richard*.

"Pearson hailed Paul Jones and shouted out, 'Have you struck your colors yet?'

"It was then that Paul Jones sent back that answer. Those were grand words, Herc. They ought to be framed and placed on board every vessel in Uncle Sam's navy."

"Yes, Paul Jones was a wonderful sea-fighter all right," agreed Herc, "but I wonder what he'd have done if he'd been cooped up in here."

"Figured on some way of getting out," rejoined Ned promptly. "Time after time British frigates hemmed him in. They thought they had him trapped. But every time he slipped through their fingers and resumed his career as a sea tiger. With his little bit of a junk-shop fleet he did more to establish the name of Americans as sea fighters than any man in the republic."

"But how about Ben Franklin, who advanced the money to buy the ships, or at least saw that it was raised?" asked the practical Herc.

"Well, of course he helped," admitted Ned, "but even he couldn't save Paul Jones from his country's ingratitude. Why, it was a hundred years or more before his bones were discovered in an obscure spot in Paris, where he died in poverty, and were brought back to this country and buried with the honors they deserved."

"Humph!" observed Herc, "that was a pretty shabby way to treat one of our biggest naval heroes. Wish we had him here now. What was that old anecdote you told me once about Paul burning his way out of a prison some place?"

"Oh, that!" laughed Ned. "I guess that was a bit of imagination on the part of the writer. At any rate it isn't mentioned in the histories.

It was one time that they locked Paul Jones in the cabin of a British vessel. They thought they had him safe. But he ripped out the lining of stuffed cushions of the captain's sofas and burned a way out through a port hole that they thought was securely locked. I read it in an old book I picked up in Philadelphia, but I guess the book was more fiction than fact."

Another silence ensued, and then Herc spoke. He took up the conversation where it had been left off.

"It's worth trying," he said in a matter-of-fact tone.

"What's worth trying?" asked Ned, through the darkness.

"Why Paul Jones' trick—or rather the trick he is supposed to have played."

"Oh, burning himself out of prison?"

"Yes."

"I don't see the connection with our case."

"Then you are a whole lot denser than I gave you credit for being."

"Thanks. But I see you've got an idea of some sort simmering in that massive brain of yours. What is it?"

"Just this, that we duplicate the trick."

"By ginger, Herc, there's nothing slow about you. You mean that we burn ourselves out of here?"

"That's just what I do. See any obstacles in the way?"

"A whole fleet of them. For one thing we'd suffocate ourselves if we tried to burn the door down, which is, I suppose, what you are driving at. Another thing—how about matches?"

"I've got lots of those. Now see here, Ned," went on Herc enthusiastically, "my plan may seem just moonshine, but it's worth trying. You know that little swinging trap at the bottom of the door?"

"Yes."

"Well, we can build our fire *outside* the door by thrusting our fuel through it and out into the passage. My idea is that the flames will rise against the surface of the door, and if we make them hot enough will burn off the bolts without setting the whole door on fire. The oak is thick enough, I think, to remove all danger of that."

"Humph!" said Ned. "There's only one thing you haven't thought of, Herc."

"What's that?"

"What are we going to build a fire with?"

"With the same stuff as Paul Jones did—or rather stuff somewhat like it—the soft lining of these padded walls."

"Say, Herc, you're a wonder! I always said you had a great brain," cried Ned banteringly, "but hasn't it occurred to you that your fire would burn out the floor of the passage and set the place on fire before it would get the bolts hot enough to make them drop off?"

"It might if the floors and walls were not concrete. I noticed them as we came along," rejoined Herc in a quiet voice.

"Herc, you ought to be director of the Smithsonian Institute or—or something big," declared

Ned admiringly. "It does begin to look as if we might have a chance to get out, after all. At any rate, it's worth trying. It will give us something to do."

"Of course it will," responded Herc cheerfully; "and now, if you'll switch on that light of yours, we'll start pulling the materials for our fire off these walls."

It didn't take long to rip out a great pile of the batting and shavings with which the walls were stuffed. These were thrust through the hole in the bottom of the door into the passage outside as fast as they were pulled out. At last the pile was declared large enough, and, with a big heap in reserve for use when the other had burned out, the boys prepared to light the mass of inflammable stuff.

It blazed up fiercely when the match was applied, but, of course, as it was outside the door in the concrete passage, the flames did not bother the boys or imperil the building. On their hands

The remaining bolt tore loose from its blackened foundations.

ON AERO SERVICE 133

and knees the two young prisoners crouched, feeding the flames assiduously when they showed signs of dying down. There was plenty of fuel, and a roaring fire was maintained.

All at once there was a soft thud outside the door, and something dropped into the flames. It was one of the heavy bolts which had torn loose from its charred and weakened fastenings. A few minutes later another crash announced that the second one had fallen.

The lads waited a few minutes, till the fire died down, and then, with beating hearts, they put their shoulders to the door.

"Heave!" roared Ned, and the next moment, under their united efforts, the remaining bolt tore loose from its blackened foundations, and the two Dreadnought Boys stood outside in the smoke-filled passage.

"Let's give three cheers!" cried Herc.

"Better be careful about making a noise," counselled Ned. "No telling but some of those rascals may be hiding in the building somewhere."

"That's right," agreed Herc. "Another thing has occurred to me, too. All the windows of this delightful place are barred, and if the door has been locked and the place vacated, we're going to have a hard time to get out, even now."

"That's right. Well, we'd better start on our tour of exploration right away."

Guided by Ned, with his torch ready for instant darkening, the two lads began to thread the maze of corridors and passages. They had been doing this for several minutes, and were beginning to get rather bewildered, when Ned stopped suddenly just as they entered a long corridor pierced with doors, with the same monotonous regularity as the others. He extinguished the light in the wink of an eye, and drew Herc swiftly into the embrasure of a doorway as he did so.

Far down the corridor a footstep had sounded, and another light had flashed. As they crouched in the darkness, prepared for any emergency, a sudden voice sounded from the end of the corridor:

"Stop right where you are, or I'll fire!"

CHAPTER XIII.

HARMLESS AS A RATTLESNAKE.

"I beg your pardon, sir, but could I speak to you a moment?"

"Certainly; come in, Chance," rejoined Lieutenant De Frees, who was sitting in his quarters on the aviation testing ground the morning after the events narrated in our last chapter.

"It's—it's about Strong and Taylor, sir, that I wished to speak," said Chance, twisting his cap in his hands. His crafty face looked more fox-like and mean than ever. His manner was almost cringing.

Lieutenant De Frees jumped to his feet.

"You've got news of them?" he exclaimed. "Out with it, my lad. They are not the boys to be absent without good reasons, although I fear that if they have overstayed their leave without just cause they must be disciplined."

"That's just it, sir," said Chance. "I—I don't want to make trouble, sir, but I'm afraid that Strong and Taylor are not all that you think them, sir. I would have spoken at roll-call this morning when they were reported absent without leave, but I thought that maybe they would turn up."

"Well, what do you know about them? Come, out with it," urged the officer sharply.

He had never liked Chance, and the seaman's furtive manner irritated him.

"Why, you see, sir, Merritt and I happened to be in town last night, sir, and we saw Strong and Taylor associating with some disreputable characters, sir. We warned them, but they laughed at us, sir. We continued to urge them to come with us, however, but they only swore at us."

"What!" exclaimed the officer, startled out of his official calm, "you saw Strong and Taylor in undesirable surroundings and with disreputable characters, and you mean to say that that is the reason for their non-appearance this morning?"

"That's just it, sir," rejoined Chance. "The last we saw of them was as they were turning into a drinking resort. I fear that some harm must have come to them, sir."

"Why—why—confound it all, I'd almost rather cut off my right hand than hear such a report, Chance. You are certain that you are correct in your report?"

"Absolutely certain, sir," was the response; "there could be no mistake. I hope I am not doing wrong in reporting this, sir?"

"No, no, my man, you have done perfectly right," was the answer, although the officer's face was troubled. The news that his most trusted pupils should have misconducted themselves had shaken him a good deal.

"Good heavens, can one place no trust in human nature?" he thought. "I'd have staked my commission that those boys were absolutely clean-lived and upright."

"Is—is there anything else you'd like to know,

sir?" Chance edged toward the door as he spoke.

"No, no. That's all, my man. You may go."

"Thank you, sir."

And Chance, his despicable errand performed, slid through the door in the same furtive way in which he had entered.

"If they haven't returned by eight bells, and there is no news of them in the meantime, I'll have to send out a picket to bring them in," mused the officer when Chance had departed. "Then disgrace and 'the brig' will follow, and two promising careers will be blasted. Strong and Taylor, of all people. I can't understand it. And yet there can be no other explanation of their absence."

Dismissing the matter from his mind for the time being, Lieutenant De Frees continued his official work. Outside on the field his subordinates attended to the morning practice of the flying squad. Half an hour must have passed thus, when a sudden knock at the door caused him to look up.

"Come in!" he said, in a sharper voice than usual. The news that his favorites had so fallen from grace had distressed him more than even he cared to own to himself.

In response to his words, the door swung open, and there, framed in the doorway, stood the two very individuals whose absence had so worried him.

Ned and Herc clicked their heels together sharply and gave the salute in a precise manner.

"We've reported on duty, sir," said Ned in a steady voice.

The officer looked at them blankly. Their clothes were torn, although an effort had seemingly been made to mend them and clean them of traces of mud and dirt. A bruise appeared on Ned's face, while Herc's hair was rumpled and standing up wildly. Their appearance bore out the story the officer had heard. Two more disreputable-looking beings it would have been hard to picture.

"So this is the way you men repay my trust

in you?" said the officer in sharp, harsh tones, very unlike his usual ones. "You will both consider yourselves under arrest, pending an inquiry. Remain standing till I summon a guard."

The lads' absolutely dumfounded looks at this reception did not escape the officer's attention.

"Well, have you any explanation to offer?" he demanded. "Mind, don't attempt to lie to me. I know all of your proceedings, dating from the hour that you, Strong, left my quarters."

"You mean that you have heard we have been engaged in some discreditable prank, sir?" asked Ned firmly, but respectfully, and still standing— as did Herc—stiffly at attention.

"I mean just that," was the response. "Since when has it been the custom in the United States navy for men to disgrace the service and go unpunished?"

"And yet," said Ned, in the same well-disciplined tones, "it hasn't been the custom to condemn men unheard, sir."

"I have heard quite enough, already," was the

sharp answer. "If you have anything to add to what Chance has told me, you may. But I warn you that any explanation you may offer will be investigated thoroughly, and if it is found you have been lying, it will go harder with you than otherwise."

"I think you will find it is Chance who has been lying, sir," said Ned calmly. "May I tell you our side of the story, dating from the hour you mentioned?"

"You may, but make it brief. My time is fully occupied," was the cold response.

But, as Ned struck into his story, telling it in a calm, even tone, the officer's expression changed from one of hard incredulity to blank astonishment, passing rapidly to deep indignation.

"We were startled soon after gaining our freedom," related Ned, going on with his narrative from the point where we left the lads, "by the sound of a voice calling on us to halt. A few minutes later we found that the man who had given the order was the local constable, Ezra

Timmons. He is a farmer on the outskirts of the town, and had been driving home late from selling some produce, when he noticed lights in the old asylum. He decided to investigate, and did so. He found the door open, and, penetrating the place, soon encountered us. He took us home with him, and helped us clean up a bit, and then we hastened over here to report."

"And that's true, by gum, every dinged word uv it!" came a voice outside the open door. Farmer—and Constable—Timmons stepped into the room, dramatically throwing back his coat and exposing a big tin star, just as he had seen constables in rural dramas do.

"But they ain't told it all," he rushed on. "These two lads here saved my wife frum some ruffians what wanted ter rob her the t'other day. They sailed by in their sky-buggy jus' in time ter save ther spoons thet Gran'ma Timmons willed me on her dyin' bed, by heck!——and it's my idee that this same gang of roustabouts was consarned in thet, frum what I kin judge."

The officer pressed a button. An orderly responded, coming smartly to attention.

"Send for Merritt and Chance at once," he ordered.

The orderly saluted and turned like an automaton.

Constable Timmons gazed at him in amazement.

"Is thet feller real or jes' one uv them clockwork dummies yer read about?" he asked.

"He's real, constable," smiled Lieutenant De Frees, with some amusement. He then began questioning the boys concerning every detail of their experiences. Nor did he forget to acknowledge that he had wronged them on the word of a rascal.

"It must have been their intention to keep you there until they had made up their minds what to do with you," he said. "But they shall not go unpunished. If a summary court martial can deal with their cases it shall do so, and at once.

ON AERO SERVICE 145

Well?" he added interrogatively, as the orderly entered the room once more.

He saluted as before, to Constable Timmons' undisguised wonder, and then said in precise tones:

"There is no trace of the men you sent for, sir."

"What!" demanded the officer.

"They were last seen leaving the grounds in an automobile, sir."

"Good heavens! This is confirmation, indeed, of their guilt," said the officer. "Were they alone?"

"No, sir. The car was driven by a person some of the men recognized as a wandering photographer who has been around the grounds for some days, sir."

"Herr Muller!" exclaimed Ned, forgetting all discipline. "I know now why the third man seemed so familiar. I—I beg your pardon, sir, but——"

"That's all right, Strong," said the officer.

"Constable, you can rely on the department co-operating with you in every way to capture these men. I can't conceive how the photographer Muller fits into the matter, but if they can be arrested we shall soon find out."

But, despite the officer's hopes of capturing the gang that had made so much trouble for Ned and Herc, they managed to conceal their traces cleverly enough to avoid arrest. The automobile in which they had taken flight—and which had been hired from a local garage—was found abandoned near a small wayside station, where they might have boarded a train for some distant point. As for the presence of the automobile, it was assumed that Herr Muller had visited the abandoned asylum early that day and discovered that the prisoners had escaped. Realizing that he must act quickly, he had evidently set out at once to warn Chance and Merritt. Incidentally, it was found out that Muller, on account of his anarchistic tendencies, had once been confined in the abandoned asylum, before its condemnation, which accounted for his familiarity with it. He had been discharged as "harmless" some time before.

"Humph! He's about as harmless as a rattlesnake!" grunted Herc, when he heard of this.

CHAPTER XIV.

FLYING FOR A RECORD.

On the day set for the flight to the *Manhattan,* which had anchored two days before in the "Roads," Ned found that he was to be the only competitor. Herc had been anxious to take part, and so had several of the other naval aviators, but Lieutenant De Frees decided that the aeroplane which Ned was to fly was the only one really suited for the work.

This aeroplane, which had been equipped with pontoons, in order to test Ned's invention, presented a peculiar appearance. Under its substructure, long, galvanized metal tanks had been fitted, in much the same way as runners are attached to a sled. The tanks were cylindrical in shape, and provided with valves, by means of which they could be "ballasted." They had been already tested and found to be suited for the work for which they were designed. They were as light as was compatible with safety, and hung far enough above the ground so as not to interfere with the landing-wheels.

A holiday from routine practice had been declared about the aviation testing grounds on the day of the daring flight. The men hung about in little groups, discussing Ned's chances of winning out in the risky feat he meant to perform. It would be the first time such a thing had ever been attempted, and they were not slow to give him full measure of praise for his daring.

The flight was to be more or less of a secret. Few on board the battleship but the naval board invited to witness the attempt, knew of the test. As a consequence, there was nobody about the grounds but the regular quota of pupils and officers when, at 10:30 a. m. the *Manhattan* wirelessed to the "Field outfit" maintained on the grounds, that all was in readiness for the trial.

A steel landing platform, made collapsible, so that it could be instantly stowed away, had been erected on the after deck of the battleship. Ned knew its approximate position, but the time had been too brief to allow him to visit the vessel and make personal observations. But if Ned realized the risk he ran in thus undertaking a flight into the practically unknown, he did not show it. In fact, he was the coolest person on the field.

At length all was in readiness, and, drawing on a pair of gauntlets, and adjusting a life-preserver, Ned stepped up to the aeroplane and clambered into his seat.

A minute later the roar of the motor, as he set it going, drowned all other sounds. But the lad caught above the uproar of the engine Lieutenant De Frees' shouted farewell:

"Good luck, my boy!"

Ned responded with a wave and a shouted cry: "Thank you, sir."

The next instant he waved his hand in token that he was ready to start. The men holding the struggling aeroplane released it, and it shot

ON AERO SERVICE 151

forward, taking the air within a few feet of the starting point. It rocketed skyward in a trail of blue smoke, leaving behind a reek of gasolene and burning lubricating oil.

Ned directed his course as high as possible, for he wished thoroughly to inspect the surroundings before he commenced his attempt. It was a bright, clear day, almost windless. As he rose higher, the glorious panorama of the open roadstead spread before his eyes. On its glistening surface lay a dark object, like a slumbering leviathan. Ned knew it in a flash for the anchored *Manhattan*—his goal.

Already a wireless had gone vibrating through the air announcing his departure, and a dozen glasses were aimed at the sky from the big fighting machine. Ned was watched for as eagerly as if he had been a real aerial enemy.

The lad circled about for a few minutes, making sure that his motor was working perfectly, and then he turned his prow toward the distant warship.

Straight toward her he flew, holding his course as true as a homing pigeon. The wind sang by his ears, and vibrated in the steel wire rigging of his sky-clipper as he raced along. The motor's drone behind him was as steady as a heart beat.

Ned's eyes shone with the desire of achievement. He was making a flight which might have a material effect upon the future armament of United States war vessels. He realized to the full the importance of his flight, and how much depended on it.

All at once his practiced eye detected, on the mirror-like surface of the stretch of water beneath him, a slight ruffle. It was some distance off. But Ned knew it spelled only one thing:

Wind!

"Bother it all," he thought, "just like the luck. However, it will only be a squall, I imagine."

He braced himself for a battle with the airman's greatest enemy. In a few seconds the squall was upon him. For an instant the aeroplane hesitated and thrilled like a live thing. Ned applied more power. Like a horse under the whip, his aeroplane shot forward. Every bolt and rivet in it strained and creaked under the tension. Ned was doing a daring thing in bucking the wind and fighting with it, instead of jockeying for some advantage.

But then Ned had a fighting nature in the best sense. An obstacle only aroused him to fresh effort. "Obstacles are things made to be conquered," he said, with another famous battler, whose name lives in history.

Zee-e-e-e-e-e-e-e-e!

The wind screamed and tore about him, while below, the water was lashed into white-caps.

"Gee whiz!" exclaimed Ned to himself. "If anything parts, I'm due to test out the floating abilities of the pontoons sooner than I expected."

But, although sadly racked and strained, the aeroplane, under her operator's skilful handling, weathered the squall. Ned turned his head and watched it go whistling and howling shoreward, with deep satisfaction.

"A fine end to the test it would have been," he muttered, "if I'd been dumped in the sea by a squall at the outset."

A few minutes later he was maneuvering above the big Dreadnought. The vessel looked queer and dwarfed from the height at which he hovered. But Ned could not help thinking what a fine object she would offer for an aerial marksman. As the lad knew, there is a limit to the perpendicular aiming of a gun, and skimming directly above the vessel, as he was, it was doubtful if the most skilful gunner on board could have hit his aeroplane.

At the stern of the big ship, the young aviator now noticed a platform—evidently the one on which he was expected to land. His heart gave a thump, as he gazed down on it.

"It doesn't look much bigger than a checkerboard," he thought, "and if I don't hit it—wow! as Herc would say."

As carefully and coolly as if he were on a practice flight, Ned regulated his levers. Then, with a quick intake of his breath, he darted downward.

Down—down, he shot, the blood singing in his ears with the rapidity of his descent. It was thrilling, desperate—dangerous!

Suddenly, as Ned placed his foot on a pedal and applied a warping appliance, there was a sharp "crack!"

The aeroplane hesitated for an instant.

Then, without the slightest warning, it lurched in sickening fashion, almost unseating him.

The next instant Ned was hurtling downward through space like a plummet. Disaster, swift and certain, rushed up to meet him from the steel fighting machine beneath.

CHAPTER XV.

A DROP FROM SPACE.

But even in that awful drop through space Ned's nerve did not desert him. His brain worked faster, in the few seconds allowed it to do effective work, than it had ever acted before.

Just as it seemed to those on board the battleship that the lad was doomed—in the event of the pontoons not working—to be drowned in the wreck of the aeroplane, they were astonished to see it recover and rise, from the very wave tips, in a graceful curve.

Straight up it shot—the motor whirring and buzzing deafeningly. Then, without an instant's hesitation, it dropped like a fish hawk toward the stern platform, and a moment later Ned Strong and his aeroplane rested on the solid foundation of the landing stage. The first flight from land to a fighting ship's deck had been successfully

ON AERO SERVICE 157

performed, with an added thrill thrown in for good measure, as it were.

Before Ned could clamber out of his seat, the officers, assembled to view the test, came crowding up on the platform. The lad was not embarrassed, but he felt a slight sense of shyness, which speedily wore off, as so many dignitaries pressed about him, shaking his hand and congratulating him.

"Jove, lad, but you gave us a fright for a minute!" exclaimed one gray-mustached captain. "I didn't think it possible that a heavier-than-air craft could recover from such a tumble as you took."

"Yes, tell us about it, lad," urged another naval dignitary.

"Well, gentlemen," said Ned, "I guess it was just one of those accidents that will happen in the best-regulated aeroplanes. Something went wrong with the warping appliances, that was all."

"Aren't your nerves shaken?" asked a young

officer. "You'd better have a glass of wine."

"Thank you, sir, I never touch alcoholic liquors," rejoined Ned simply. "But I wouldn't mind a glass of water, sir. Flying is rather thirsty work."

An orderly was at once dispatched for a carafe and a glass, and while he was gone Ned obtained leave to locate and repair the break that had come so close to causing him disaster. It was soon found, and a new turnbuckle put on in place of the one that had cracked when a flaw in its construction parted.

By this time every jackie who could find business in the after part of the ship was on the decks below. A sea of faces was upturned to gaze at the flying marvel.

Questions flew thick and fast.

"Would it be possible to carry a sharpshooter, for instance, from the deck of this vessel, circle a hostile craft and return?" asked one of the naval officers standing about.

"I think so, sir," was Ned's response.

"Well, providing you feel there is no danger, why not try such an experiment?" asked Commander Dunham, Ned's old chief officer.

"I should like to, above all things, sir," rejoined Ned, with sparkling eyes; "but who will go?"

"I think you will have no lack of volunteers," smiled Commander Dunham, as half a dozen young ensigns and midshipmen pressed forward. "Mr. Shrike, I think you are as good a subject as any. At any rate, sir, your weight will not seriously embarrass the craft."

Mr. Shrike proved to be an extremely thin young midshipman, whose weight, as Commander Dunham had humorously hinted, was not excessive. In fact, among his intimates he was known as "The Shrimp."

He lost no time in preparing for the ride, providing himself with a light rifle. When all was in readiness, Ned showed him where to sit, and how to hold on, and then, the aeroplane having already been swung about, he started up the engine once more. Several blue-jackets had been detailed to hold the machine back, and at a given signal from Ned they let go. The aeroplane shot from the platform out over the stern of the battleship, and soared out above the sea. As they shot past Old Glory, waving proudly at the stern, Ned saluted with one hand. The young middy at his side followed his example.

The aeroplane took a perilous swoop as she dropped from the platform, but Ned had his craft well in hand. He averted the drop with a quick movement and speedily swung out seaward.

"See, there is a small sloop off there," said Midshipman Shrike presently. "Let's try if we can circle it, just as if it were a hostile vessel."

"Very well, sir," rejoined Ned, and steered straight for a white sail glistening some distance out at sea.

Closer and closer they drew to it, and before long they could see men on its deck pointing upward excitedly.

"They've seen us, anyway," laughed the middy. "Wonder if they think we're some big sort of a gull?"

Suddenly, as they drew closer to the sloop, Ned saw one of the men go in the cabin for a moment and emerge with a gun—or at least something that looked like one.

"Hullo! What's that fellow doing now?" asked Midshipman Shrike, as he saw this. "Is that a gun he has there, Strong?"

"Looks like it, sir," rejoined Ned, "and he's——"

"Aiming at us, by Jove! Hi, there, you rascal, put that gun down!"

A puff of smoke came simultaneously with the words. It was followed by a screaming sound, as a bullet whizzed past the aerial voyagers. It was followed by another and another, the rifle evidently being a repeater.

"I say, I can't stand this any longer," shrilled the middy, as Ned kept the aeroplane swinging in rapid circles. As he spoke, he jerked the rifle to his shoulder, and, with a cry of "Stop that shooting instantly!" fired a shot across the sloop's bow. Ned could see the white water whipped up as the bullet ricochetted.

But, in firing his weapon, the young officer had released his hold with both hands. At the same instant a puff of wind swung the aeroplane sharply on her beam ends. Ned righted her instantly, but, as he did so, he was horrified to observe that he was alone.

The sharp lurch had dislodged his companion, and below Ned saw him whirling downward. The midshipman's body struck the water close by the sloop and instantly vanished.

With the automatic movements of one in a nightmare, Ned dropped downward. As he did so, he was immensely relieved to see the young officer's head bob up to the surface for an instant. Ned shouted and an answering hail came upward.

"Thank heaven, I've got the pontoons on," he thought.

But even while his mind and body were thus busied, Ned had time to observe the sloop. She had taken advantage of the puff of wind, and was now rapidly slipping off toward a not far distant point of land. Ned's eye took in her every detail. She was black and squat, yet with a certain raciness of line, and heavily canvassed. Round her bulwarks ran a bright crimson line. She bore no name that Ned could see.

The aeroplane struck the water with a splash that threw the spray high above her planes. But the pontoons saved her from being submerged. A moment after she had struck the surface of the water she was floating like a sea-bird on its surface.

"Ahoy, there!" came a hail.

Ned glanced in the direction and saw the young middy striking out boldly for the floating aeroplane.

"Hurt, sir?" demanded Ned.

"Not a bit; the water's fine," was the cheery

response. "But, confound it all, I've lost my rifle."

Ned swung the aeroplane round, using the regular aerial propellers to drive her over the water. It was not many minutes before a dripping but cheerful middy was seated once more by his side.

"I say, Strong," he remarked, "I guess the less said about this adventure the better. You understand. I had no business to fire at those chaps on the sloop, as a matter of fact, but I couldn't help it. What do you think they fired at us for?"

"I've no idea, sir," was Ned's reply.

"Guess they were crazy, or had been drinking, or something."

"Possibly that was it, Mr. Shrike." But in the Dreadnought Boy's mind he had reached a far different conclusion. The shots that whistled about them had not been aimed by any irresponsible hand, of that he was sure. They had been aimed to do harm. That they had not succeeded was due to good fortune more than anything else. There were only certain men whom Ned could think of who could be guilty of such an outrage. Those men were the implacable enemies of himself and Herc.

"Better cruise about a bit till I get dried out," said the middy presently. "If they ask us why we dropped like that, I'll say we were trying out the pontoons, eh?"

Ned agreed. He did not countenance untruths or an approach to them, as a rule, but in this case he felt that to tell the whole story might get Midshipman Shrike in trouble, as well as involve him in some difficulties. However, he resolved that if questions were asked, he would tell the truth, as he would then have no other recourse. But, to his relief, no interrogations were put to him, and he supposed that the midshipman had explained the case, as was, indeed, the fact.

Soon after their return, Ned winged back to the shore. Here he was the recipient of more congratulations, but his mind was busy elsewhere than with his signal triumph in aerial navigation. As soon as he got a chance, he sought out Herc. The astonishment of the freckle-faced Dreadnought Boy, on hearing the news, may be imagined.

"Then you are sure that it was Muller and that crowd?" he asked.

"Practically certain," rejoined Ned. "Who else would have done such a thing?"

"Do you think they have some rendezvous in the neighborhood?"

"I'm sure of it. Their possession of the sloop indicates that. I'd like to unearth their hiding-place and put the rascals to rout."

"So would I," agreed Herc, "and maybe we will. At any rate, that sloop should be easy to identify."

"Yes. We'll keep a bright lookout, and perhaps before long we may have something tangible to work on."

That time was to come sooner than they expected.

CHAPTER XVI.

THE SETTING OF A TRAP.

"I've just received a telegram that a freight wreck has tied up our new motors and spare aeroplane parts at Bartonville," said Lieutenant De Frees, one afternoon a few days after Ned's adventures with the pontoon-fitted aeroplane.

"Most annoying," responded the ensign with whom he was talking. "We need them in a hurry, too."

"That's so. I guess I'll have to send a couple of men after them. There is a big auto truck at Bartonville. I remember it, because it brought out some stuff for us before. It can easily carry the delayed parts. Strong and Taylor have been working pretty hard lately. I guess a little trip will do them good. I'll send them. At any rate, I'll know I can depend upon them."

"That's right. They are two of the most

promising lads I've ever seen. By the way, has anything further ever been heard of those rascals who tried to discredit them?"

"Not a word. But the secret service reports that this man Muller, as he calls himself, is known in Europe as a most dangerous anarchist. The fellow is, in fact, a maniac on the subject."

"Ha! I suppose we can call ourselves lucky that he didn't blow us all up. Those anarchist chaps are bitterly opposed to all navies and armies, and some of the worst of them have even attempted to destroy transatlantic liners."

"Yes, I read in the paper the other day about an infernal machine having been found among the cargo of a large vessel just as she was about to sail for Europe. By the way, of course you heard about the clever manner in which Strong and Taylor prevented the destruction of the submarine?"

"I did hear something about it, but not the full story, I fancy. Would you mind telling it?"

"Not in the least. But first let me send for

Strong and Taylor. I'll despatch them on their errand at once. They will have to get a rig and drive over. Bartonville is ten miles away, and they may experience some delay when they arrive there."

Thus it came about that that afternoon Ned and Herc found themselves in Bartonville, registered as guests at the Bartonville House. As the lieutenant had anticipated, they experienced some delay in getting permission to transship the goods from the delayed freight train. But the magic word "Navy" soon smoothed out all obstacles. It would be necessary for them to wait till the following day, however, before finishing up their business. Ned's first duty was to send a telegram to Lieutenant De Frees to that effect. In return he received orders for both Herc and himself to remain and see the business through.

"Well," grinned Herc, as the two lads sat in the lobby of the hotel in soft leather-upholstered chairs, "this is certainly solid comfort for a pair of petty officers."

"It's a long cry from here to the forecastle of the *Manhattan,* and that's a fact," admitted Ned. "But somehow I'd rather be on duty than lounging around here."

"Oh, bother duty," blurted out Herc, "when first we entered the navy, it was always duty— although that duty was mostly scrubbing decks, painting and cleaning brasswork. And now it's duty still, and——"

"So it will be to the end, old fellow," said Ned seriously. "Everyone in the navy has his duty to attend to, too. Wasn't it attention to duty that won Manila Bay, and duty that took Farragut—— Great Scott!"

The lads had been sitting facing the street near a big plate glass window. The sight that had brought Ned to his feet with such a sharp exclamation was the momentary glimpse of a familiar face passing on the street.

"Wait here for me for a while, Herc," he said. "I'll be back directly."

"What—why?" spluttered Herc, but before

he could voice any more interrogations, Ned dashed from the room with the swiftness of a skyrocket, and, jamming his hat on his head, was out of the doors of the hotel in a flash, almost upsetting the porter in his haste. Herc sprang after him, but before he gained the doorway Ned was round the corner and hopelessly lost. Herc retraced his steps to the hotel and resumed his seat.

It was something like an hour later that he heard his name called through the lobby by a bell-boy. He hastened to the desk and the clerk motioned toward an ill-kempt looking man who was standing there.

"Mr. Taylor?" asked this individual.

"That's me," responded the rough-and-ready Herc, with a grin.

"I've a message for you from Mr. Strong," went on the other. "He wishes you to come to him at once."

Herc's suspicions were aroused in an instant.

Perhaps this was a trap of some sort. He resolved to be cautious.

"Where is he?" he asked.

The man beckoned him to one side.

"I don't want everybody to hear our business," he said. "Your chum has succeeded in locating that rascally band of Muller's. They are at a place on the outside of the town. You and I will go to him in a hack, that was his message."

The man seemed sincere, but Herc was still inclined to doubt him."

"Where did you meet my shipmate?" he asked.

"Why, I'm a fisherman on the headwaters of the bay that runs up into Bartonville," was the rejoinder, with every appearance of frankness. "Your chum didn't want to leave the place where he had spotted the band, so he sent me after you and told me that you'd give me some money for my trouble."

This request for money lulled Herc's suspicions at once. Had the man not asked for it, the thing might have looked suspicious, but the fact that he expected to be rewarded for coming with the message seemed to indicate that he was honest and above board. But he had one more question to ask.

"Wouldn't it be a good plan to notify the police?" he said.

"He told me to do that," replied the man. "I stopped in at the station on the way up, and a patrol-wagon full of cops has started. We'll have to go fast to catch them."

Herc searched his pockets. But, as luck would have it, he could not find more than a few bits of silver. But the boys on their arrival had deposited in the hotel safe the money entrusted to them to pay their expenses, and also to defray the charges on the freighted goods. Herc recollected this, and thinking that it might be a good plan to have some money along, he withdrew a considerable part of their funds. Had he caught the glitter in the man's eyes, he would have been warned.

"Now, I'm ready," he said, as he thrust the money into his breast pocket.

"All right, guv'ner," was the response, "the carriage is right outside."

Herc, following his conductor, soon found himself inside a closed hack drawn by two horses. The messenger said something to the coachman and then threw himself in beside Herc. The carriage at once moved off at a rapid pace. Bartonville was not a very large place, and the town and its scattering outskirts were speedily left behind. The carriage began to roll and bump along over country roads.

"How far off is the place?" Herc kept asking, and each time he was assured that it was "only a little way further."

At last the carriage stopped on a deserted bit of roadway.

"Here's where we get out," said Herc's conductor, "we'll have to hike it across that field and through that bit of woods before we get to your pal."

Herc paid the coachman and the man at once drove off.

"This way," said the man, climbing over a rail fence and striking off across a field, on the further side of which was a patch of ragged woods. Through the trees Herc could catch the glint of water.

It was a lonely spot. He looked about him, but could not see any trace of a human habitation.

"If this should be a trap I'm nicely in it, all right," he muttered to himself as he followed his guide into the shadows of the wood.

"How much further?" he asked, as they stumbled along over the rough path.

"Right ahead down by the creek," said the man. "We're almost there now."

With a few paces more they emerged on the banks of a slow-flowing and muddy creek, which was evidently tidal and joined the Bartonville Bay lower down. About a hundred yards off stood a rickety looking shack, and anchored in the creek opposite to it was a sloop with a red band painted round its bulwarks. Suddenly and for no reason that he could assign, the recollection flashed across Herc that he had heard Ned speak of such a sloop. At the time though he could not recall in what connection.

"Is this the place?" asked Herc, as his guide slackened his pace.

"This is it," nodded the man, and again a sharp presentiment that all was not right, flashed through Herc. But it was too late to hold back now.

"I'll give him the signal," said the man, placing his fingers to his lips. A shrill whistle followed.

As if by magic, from the tall, spiky grass about them, half a dozen men sprang erect.

"It is a trap!" shouted Herc, flinging himself furiously upon the first man who rushed at him. The lad fought valiantly, but the contest was too uneven to last long. Within five minutes, Herc, raging like a lion, and inwardly abusing his own gullibility that had led him into such an ambush, was bound hand and foot and stretched a prisoner on the floor of the old rookery of a shanty.

CHAPTER XVI.

THE SPRINGING THEREOF.

The rude hut, which, judging by its odor and condition, was used as an occasional shelter for the bay fishermen, was full of talk and smoke. Herc could not catch much meaning from the confused babel of tongues, but judged from the intelligible snatches he could seize upon, that it related to himself and Ned.

He was hardly surprised to recognize, among the occupants of the place, Chance and Merritt, as well as Herr Muller. There were four or five other men, including the one who had led him into the trap.

Herc's keen eyes also noticed one peculiarity about each of the men about him. Every one of them wore in his buttonhole a tiny strip of bright red ribbon. What its significance might be, he had no way of telling, of course, but it impressed him.

"Well," said Herr Muller at last, his voice rising masterfully above those of the rest, "we had better be getting on board. The tide is on the turn, and we have much to do. Besides, they may pursue us from the town."

"No chance of that, comrade," rejoined the man who had conducted Herc from Bartonville. "I got the lad away without any one noticing our departure."

"Just the same, both those Dreadnought Boys are tricky as cats," snarled Merritt. "My advice is to get away at once."

A general bustle followed. Herc was lifted bodily, and carried down a narrow plank gangway leading to the sloop. Once on board, he was half-thrown, half-pushed, into a stuffy cabin, and the door above him closed with a sharp bang. He heard a metallic clang, as the bolts and lock, which evidently held it, were closed.

"Wow!" exclaimed the Dreadnought Boy. "If

this isn't what old Ben Franklin would call 'the logical limit of the uttermost.' "

The cabin was almost dark, being lighted only by two dirty and very small port holes. It was, moreover, stuffy and malodorous. Herc tried to get on his feet, but, being bound hand and foot, he was compelled to lie as he had fallen at the foot of the stairs. On deck he could hear the trampling of feet, and before long the motion of the sloop told him that she was under way.

"Going to sea, I guess," mused Herc. "I wonder what they mean to do with me?"

He was left to speculate on this topic for some time. The motion of a choppy sea was already manifest when a man descended into the cabin with some bread and some cold meat. He also had a stone jug presumably containing water.

"Here you are," he said, thrusting it in front of Herc. "You'd better eat while you get a chance."

"I can't do that very well while I'm all trussed up like a roasting chicken," objected Herc.

ON AERO SERVICE 181

"That's so," assented the man. "Well, I guess there's no harm in setting you loose for a while. We've cleared the bay, and the only place you can go to if you want to get away is overboard."

So saying, he loosened Herc's bonds, to the immense satisfaction of the freckle-faced boy.

The man seemed to be a shade less rough than his companions, so Herc ventured to ask him a question.

"What is the occasion for all this?" he inquired in a half-humorous tone.

"Now, don't ask questions, and you won't hear untruths," said the man.

With this, he hastened out of the cabin, carefully relocking the companionway door on the outside.

"Wow!" exclaimed Herc, giving vent to his favorite exclamation. Then he fell to eating with a will.

The meal, coarse as it was, revived his spirits. It was only when he came to taste the water that he put it down with a wry face. It was bitter, and had a nauseating flavor.

"I'm not certain," mused Herc, "but nevertheless, I'm pretty sure that some sort of drug has been placed in that stuff. Too bad. I'm thirsty enough to drink it all, too."

The motion of the sloop was quite lively now. It was evident that they were some distance out at sea. Occasionally, too, a green wave, washing over one of the port-holes, partially obscured what little light there was.

"Guess I might as well explore the place and see what sort of a craft this is," said Herc, as inactivity grew irksome. He started up from the locker on which he had been sitting, and made toward a door at the stern of the cabin.

It was not locked, and the lad threw it open without effort. What was his astonishment to see, stretched on a bunk, apparently in deep slumber, the form of his missing comrade.

"Ned! Ned!" exclaimed Herc, springing forward.

ON AERO SERVICE

Usually Ned, as sailors say, "slept with one eye open." This was a quality he shared with most seamen.

Herc was heartily astonished, therefore, to find that his shipmate did not respond at once to his vigorous shakings and shoutings. At length however, he bestirred himself, and yawned, moving in an inert fashion, much unlike his usual movements, which were full of activity and life.

"Oh-ho! Hi-hum!" he yawned, gaping broadly, and gazing about him. "What's up, watch turning out?"

"Wish it was, and that we were safe back on the old *Manhattan*," muttered Herc.

"No, my hearty," he went on, "the watch isn't being turned out; but it's time you woke up, just the same. It's my opinion that you've been drugged with some of that stuff they tried to give me."

After renewed efforts, Herc finally succeeded in getting Ned broad awake. But it was some minutes before his befogged brain took in the situation. As Herc had suspected, he had been drugged by some substance placed in a drink of water he had asked for.

Ned, once restored to himself, speedily explained how it was the sight of Kennell passing the hotel that had caused him to make his hasty exit, and indirectly bring about the present situation.

He had followed Kennell through the outskirts of the town, he said, wishing to find out where he was going. He succeeded in this beyond his hopes, but Kennell, it appeared subsequently, had been aware that Ned was following him, from the moment the Dreadnought Boy had left the hotel. Cunningly he had led him right up to the lone fisher hut, and Ned's capture had been swift and easy for the nefarious band.

Herc's story followed.

"There's something mysterious about the band," he said. "Take that bit of ribbon they wear, for instance—what is it? What does it signify?"

"I heard enough of their talk before I drank the drugged water to apprise me of that," said Ned. "These fellows are a bunch of desperate anarchists. They are acting, as far as I can make out, in the interests of some European power, and mean to do all the harm they can to Uncle Sam's navy."

"The despicable scoundrels!" gasped Herc. "But how did Chance and Merritt come to join them?"

"Money, I suppose. They seem to be well supplied. I guess Chance and Merritt are being well paid for the information they can impart to the rascals concerning the secrets of our naval organization."

"Do you think it is possible they could be such traitors?"

"Anything is possible where they are concerned. By the way, Herc, this is no ordinary sloop we are on. In the first place, it is the same craft as that from which I was fired on at the time Midshipman Shrike fell from the aeroplane."

Herc nodded.

"Now I know why that red stripe seemed so familiar," he said.

"Moreover," resumed Ned, "she is fitted with wireless."

"With wireless!"

"Yes. The instruments are in another cabin forward of this one. I noticed the aerial wires on her mast, too, as I was brought on board. Muller ordered them hauled down, but not before I had seen them."

"What does she want with a wireless apparatus?"

"I can't imagine, unless it is to catch the messages that the ships of the navy are sending concerning plans, and so on."

"But they are in cipher."

"Yes, but there are two men on board who know that cipher—Chance and Merritt. That fact alone explains their value to the anarchists."

"Humph! That's so," agreed Herc. "But what's the matter with our looking about a bit more? We might discover something else."

"All right. My head still aches a little, but otherwise I'm well enough," responded Ned. "I guess we are safe from interruption for a time. The wind seems to be freshening, and the men will all be busy on deck. I reckon they think we are both drugged, too, and are safe not to awaken for some time."

"Wow! I'm glad I didn't drink that water, or there would be more truth than poetry in that," said Herc.

"I guess they gave me a light dose, for I didn't taste it," said Ned.

"Good thing they did, or I couldn't have roused you so easily."

The two boys cautiously set about exploring the cabin. It was a bare little place, and did not contain much subject matter for investigation. There was a door forward leading to the wireless room, but it was locked. Ned listened at the keyhole, but the instruments were silent.

"Hullo!" said Herc, suddenly halting and pointing downward at the cabin floor. "What's under here, I wonder?"

There was a ring at his feet. Ned lost no time in laying hold of it. He gave it a sharp tug, and it came up easily, bringing with it a section of flooring to which it had been attached.

It revealed a dark, yawning space under the cabin floor, into which both boys peered eagerly.

"There's something in there, but I can't make out what," said Ned presently. "Wait a jiffy, till I strike a match."

A lucifer was soon lighted, and Ned, bending over, held it inside the hole in the cabin floor. He recoiled with a jump and a suppressed cry, as if he had suddenly discovered a nest of rattlesnakes.

"What's up?" demanded Herc, who had been able to detect nothing but a metallic glitter, like that of steel.

"Torpedoes!" gasped Ned; "six Whiteheads! enough to destroy all the finest and newest vessels of Uncle Sam's navy."

CHAPTER XVII.

ON BOARD THE SLOOP.

They had no further opportunity, just then, to comment on their discovery. For, just as Ned voiced it, somebody could be heard fumbling with the lock on the companionway door. It was the work of an instant for Herc to replace the removable section of the flooring while Ned slid silently and swiftly back into the cabin he had vacated.

Herc had just time to resume his seat on the locker, together with a vacant expression of countenance, when the door was flung open. It admitted a gust of fresh, crisp air and a shower of spray.

"Wish I was up on deck inhaling some of that," commented Herc to himself, as he turned his head to see who the newcomer might be.

It proved to be Herr Muller. He came down

the steps slowly, glancing about him sharply as he came. He seemed somewhat surprised as his eyes lit on Herc perched up on his locker.

"Ah, ha! awake!" he exclaimed.

"You hadn't any reason to suppose I'd be asleep, had you?" inquired Herc blandly.

"No. You boys are too wide-awake altogether. That is why we have taken you off on this cruise," chuckled the anarchist grimly.

"Very considerate of you, I'm sure," rejoined Herc. "And this—this cruise, I presume, it isn't for our health?"

"Hardly," rejoined the other, with a smile; "I mean to make you useful to us and—to the cause!"

His eyes glittered as he spoke. The glare of a fanatic filled them.

"How is your comrade?" he asked the next instant.

Herc saw the trap instantly. Muller had thought to trap him into answering without thought. Had he done so, the crafty anarchist would have known that the boys had been talking together. So Herc assumed his most unworldly expression.

"What, is Ned on board?" he exclaimed.

"You didn't know it?"

"Not I. You are clever fellows to have trapped both of us."

Herr Muller looked at the lad sharply. He did not know what to make of this careless, debonair manner.

"Well, as you observed," he said at length, "we have trapped you."

"But what for? What do you want with little us?" grinned Herc.

"You are making fun of me, Mister Yankee."

"Not any more fun than you make of yourself," parried Herc quickly.

Herr Muller looked more puzzled than ever. Then he frowned suddenly. "You do not seem to realize the seriousness of your position," he said.

"Not I. Oh, I'm a care-free sail-o-r-r-r-r oh!"

sang Herc. "How do you like my singing?" he inquired.

"Not very much," replied the other, looking at him with the same puzzled expression. Herr Muller couldn't make out whether Herc was crazy or simply light-headed.

"Sorry you don't like it," rejoined Herc; "when I sing in big cities it brings crowds. Sometimes it brings the police."

"I don't wonder. But I did not come down here to talk nonsense. Where is your companion?"

"I told you before I didn't know," rejoined Herc, seemingly with all the carelessness in the world. For the second time the crafty foreign anarchist had failed to trap Herc into an admission that he and Ned had met.

"I'll go and get him," said Herr Muller, starting for the cabin.

"I wish you'd bring me a glass of water," said Herc.

"There is water in that stone jug," said Herr Muller, indicating the drugged receptacle.

"Oh, I drank all that a long time ago," rejoined Herc, "I'm very fond of water."

For a reason we know of, Herr Muller looked surprised.

"You drank *all* that water!" he exclaimed.

"Sure," rejoined Herc.

"Our water supply has run rather low," said Herr Muller, watching the Dreadnought Boy narrowly, "did you notice anything peculiar about that water?"

"Ah, now you come to speak of it, I did notice a peculiar taste to it," said Herc, restraining a desire to chuckle at the other's amazement, "a sort of bitter flavor. Is it that which you refer to?"

"Perhaps. But—but didn't it make you sleepy?" queried the other, his curiosity overcoming his discretion.

"Never felt more wide awake in my life," responded Herc, "I could sing this instant. I——"

ON AERO SERVICE 195

But Herr Muller had fled into Ned's cabin. He found the boy apparently just wakening from a sound slumber, although Ned had enjoyed every word of Herc's foolish banter.

"Ah, so you are awake at last, Mister Sailor," said Herr Muller; "may I trouble you to come into the other cabin? I have business of importance to discuss."

"I beg your pardon," said Ned shortly.

"What do you mean?"

"Just this: that I have no business to discuss with a scoundrel."

The reply was like the crack of a whip. The other grew livid.

"Be careful how you speak," he said, striving to retain control of himself, "I am not accustomed to being made game of by whipper-snappers."

"Well, what do you want?" asked Ned, feeling that, after all, he might learn something by pretending to fall in with the rascal's plans, whatever they might prove to be.

"Then you are willing to talk business with us?"

"That depends," rejoined Ned, "on whether it's profitable business. But I warn you," he went on, raising his voice, "my comrade and I want to be paid in full and well, too, for anything we do."

Herc in the outer cabin heard the heightened tones.

"What's Ned up to now?" he wondered to himself, "I'll bet he's hit on some plan. I guess that whatever he says I'll follow his lead. I don't like playing at being a traitor, though, just the same."

Herr Muller and Ned now emerged into the outer cabin.

"Sit down," said the anarchist, pointing to a place beside Herc. Both boys instantly simulated great delight and surprise at seeing each other. Herr Muller looked on somewhat glumly.

"I wonder if they are making fools of me," he thought. "They are both sharp as steel traps, as they say in this country. It is possible. Well, I shall govern myself accordingly and watch them closely."

"Well," said Ned, when the first apparently warm greetings were over, "what is it you want us to do?"

"Just this," said Herr Muller, "you are a good mechanic and a fair draughtsman. I want you to draw me a sectional design of the *Manhattan*. When that is done I've got other work for you to do."

"A design of the *Manhattan?*" repeated Ned slowly as if he had not quite understood. He was in reality trying to gain time to think.

"Yes. You are familiar with her, and I believe she is the finest ship of your navy."

"I can say 'yes,' to both questions," rejoined Ned. "What would you want this drawing to show?"

"For one thing, I should like to know where her armor is thinnest," was the rejoinder.

Herr Muller's eyes narrowed as he spoke, and he gazed sharply at the lad before him.

"You understand?" he asked, as Ned did not reply.

"Perfectly. I was just trying to collect my thoughts. So you want a sectional plan of the *Manhattan,* showing where her armor is thinnest," he said slowly. "Well, supposing I make one, what is there in it for me?"

"That depends on the success of the grand project," was the rejoinder.

Ned looked puzzled. Into the anarchist's eyes there had come the same glare of fanatical fire that Herc had noted there before.

"What is this grand project, if I may ask?" he said presently.

"You may ask," was the reply, "but I shall not answer. The accomplishment itself shall be your reply—and the world's."

The man had risen to his feet and was pacing up and down the cabin excitedly. Suddenly he turned sharply.

"I shall ask for your reply in half an hour," he said abruptly, and plunged, rather than mounted, up the cabin stairs.

Ned sat lost in thought after his departure. After a long period of speechlessness, Herc spoke.

"What are you thinking about, Ned?" he asked.

"I'm trying to put two and two together," said Ned softly. "If I'm right in my conclusions, this fellow Muller is one of the most diabolical scoundrels that ever encumbered the face of the earth."

CHAPTER XIX.

"BY WIRELESS!"

"Ye-es," drawled Herc judicially, "even without putting two and two together, I must say that I agree with you. But what particular brand of mischief is he up to now, do you think?"

"Well, in the first place, he doesn't want the plans of the *Manhattan* just because of his interest in naval architecture."

"No, hardly. But it gets me what he does want them for."

"I've formed a pretty definite idea," rejoined Ned. "It was those torpedoes that set me thinking. Herc, I believe that a gigantic plot to injure the American navy is on foot. Those torpedoes are aboard to be used in pursuance of that purpose."

"Jiminy crickets!" yelled Herc, fairly brought to his feet; "and you talk about it as calmly as if you were asking me to come and have an ice-cream soda. By the same token, if I don't get something to drink pretty soon I'll dry up and wither away."

"We've got to keep calm," rejoined Ned. "Getting excited won't do any good. Look here, Herc, have you anything in the shape of a wrench about you?"

"I've got that small one I use on the motor of my aeroplane."

"Not any too big," commented Ned. "But it'll have to do. Now, Herc, you watch the stairway while I get busy."

"If any one comes down, shall I tackle them?" asked the freckle-faced youth, who was always ready for a rough-and-tumble.

"Good gracious, no! To arouse their suspicions that we are anything but friendly to them would never do. Just tell me if you hear any one fumbling with the door."

"All right," said Herc, taking up his position at the foot of the stairway.

Ned at once yanked up the section of flooring operated by the ring. By dint of wriggling and twisting, he managed to work himself down into the compartment containing the deadly implements. Then he set to work with his wrench.

The task kept him busy for half an hour or more. When he finally emerged from his cramped quarters into the cabin, he carried something very carefully wrapped in his handkerchief. Whatever it was, he threw it out of the cabin port and breathed a sigh of relief when he had done so. Two more trips were necessary before the flooring was replaced, and each time Ned threw something out.

Herc was about to ask his comrade what he was doing, when the preliminary fumbling at the bolts above warned him that they were about to have a visitor.

Instantly both lads resumed the same positions they had occupied when Herr Muller left the cabin. They had just time to assume them when the man himself opened the companionway doorway and descended.

"Well, have you made up your minds?" he began, without any preliminaries.

"We have," replied Ned. "I'll do as you wish in regard to the plan of the battleship. But you haven't mentioned anything about compensation as yet."

"It will be large. You have my word for that. Isn't that enough?"

Ned, inwardly thinking that it certainly wasn't, agreed that it was.

"I'll get you pencils and paper, and you can set to work right away," said Herr Muller.

But just as he spoke there came a loud crash on deck, and a series of alarmed shouts. Herr Muller turned and sprang quickly back up the stairway. The boys, feeling certain that some calamity had occurred, followed him.

As they gained the deck they were astonished to find that the sloop was out of sight of land. A desolate expanse of gray, tumbling billows was stretched about her. But their glances only dwelt on this for an instant. Their immediate attention was caught by a group in the stern, bending over a prostrate figure.

"It's Chance!" exclaimed Ned, hastening aft, followed by Herc.

"A block tore loose from above and struck him on the head," one of the followers of Herr Muller was explaining as the boys came up.

The leader of the strange band bent over the unconscious man and felt his head with a manner that betokened some medical skill.

"It is only a flesh wound," he said, "but the shock has made him unconscious. Carry him below, some of you. He'll soon be all right again."

Kennell was one of those who volunteered for this service. Merritt was another. As they passed the two boys, carrying their limp burden, Kennell turned to Ned:

"Well, my young sneak, they've got you

collared this time," he said with a leer, "you walked into the trap like a baby taking candy."

Ned did not deign to reply to the fellow. Instead, he listened to Herr Muller who was talking excitedly.

"Of all unlucky things to happen at this time," he was saying. "We shall be within the wireless zone of the fleet at any time now, and the only man on board who understands wireless is incapacitated. It is most unfortunate."

A sudden idea came to Ned. Possibly by volunteering to act in Chance's place he might find a way out of the maze that involved them.

Acting on his impulse he stepped up to Muller.

"I understand wireless," he said; "what messages do you want taken?"

"I don't know yet," rejoined Herr Muller, looking much relieved. Then suddenly his manner changed.

"But you understand the naval code, too, don't you?"

The manner in which the question was worded

put Ned on his guard. He saw that it would be better to reply in the negative.

"No," he said, shaking his head, "I haven't had much to do with the signal part of man-o'-war work; but, of course, I learned something of wireless at the naval school."

"Good!" exclaimed Herr Muller; "come with me."

He ushered the boys below—for Herc had trailed along—and into the small wireless room Ned had noticed.

"I am expecting a message at any time now," he said; "but it will come in cipher. Get it absolutely accurate and you will not suffer by it."

Ned nodded.

"Better see about hoisting your aerials," he said.

Herr Muller hurried off on this errand, while Ned looked over the instruments surrounding him. They glistened with brass and polished steel in the smoky light of a bulkhead lamp. But despite the evident haste with which they had been installed, it was easy to see that the apparatus was the finest obtainable.

"What on earth can be up now?" wondered Herc, as Ned took up the metal headpiece and adjusted it.

"Don't know yet," said Ned. "It's evident, though, that Muller is in hopes of picking up some information from the fleet by eavesdropping on its wireless. I'm mighty glad now that I didn't tell him I could read cipher."

Further conversation was interruped by the re-entrance of Herr Muller. He stepped brusquely up to Ned.

"You had better be ready to catch anything you can," he said; "everything is in readiness above, and we should be picking up messages at any moment now."

Ned nodded and sat down on the stool set over against the table, on which the glittering array of instruments were fastened.

For a long time—or so it seemed to him—he sat thus. Suddenly, in his ears, there sounded the faintest of scratching sounds. It was as soft as the footsteps of an invalid fly. But Ned knew that somewhere out on the sea ship was speaking to ship, and that what he heard was the echo of their talk.

Suddenly he picked up a pencil and began to write rapidly. Herr Muller bent over his shoulder. He watched with keen absorption as Ned's pencil flew over the paper.

"Yes, she's all right; but she's not as pretty as the blonde operator at Key West."

"Is that the message you were expecting?" inquired Ned blandly, gazing up at Herr Muller.

"What nonsense is dot?" sputtered the other, lapsing into his foreign accent.

"Well, since you ask me," rejoined Ned, "I think it's the operator on one coasting steamer talking to the wireless man on another vessel about a blonde young lady at Key West."

Herr Muller exploded.

"Vot I care aboudt blonde young vimins?" he demanded, pounding the table angrily. "Der message I vant iss a navy message, you onderstond dot?"

"Oh, that's it, is it?" inquired Ned, assuming great innocence. "I thought you wanted every message that came through the air.—Hullo!—Hush!—Here she comes now!"

Suddenly a new note had struck into the wireless channels. The quick, imperious call of a battleship summoning the wireless ears of another sea-fighter.

"M-n! M-n! M-n!"

"It's the *Manhattan* being called by the flagship," muttered Ned. "Hullo! now they're answering."

"Squadron will rendezvous at Blackhaven Bay. Will await further instructions there," he translated rapidly. But his translation was mental only. To Herr Muller he handed only a string of figures, the cipher the two vessels had been using. Muller hastened off with it to Chance's cabin. The man had now recovered from his

swoon and might be able to translate the message.

Ned took instant advantage of the situation.

With quick, nervous fingers he began pounding the sending key. The lithe, white spark crackled and flashed across the terminals. It crackled like a bunch of firecrackers.

"*M-n! M-n! M-n!*" was what the boy kept pounding out.

Would the *Manhattan* never answer?

The spark crackled on, but no answering flash came through the air.

"The apparatus is too weak," groaned Ned, despairing at the long silence. But at the same instant his heart gave a great pound. His pulses began to leap. Through space had come an answering message.

Ned lost no time. His fingers began to pound the sending key once more.

"*Danger. At Blackhaven*——"

Bang!

The interruption was sharp and startling.

In the doorway stood Merritt, revolver in hand.

Splinters flew from under Ned's fingers as the bullet smashed the sending key to smithereens. He turned swiftly. In the doorway stood Merritt, revolver in hand. It was the recreant seaman who had fired the shot and interrupted Ned's warning message.

"So you thought you'd tip us off to the *Manhattan*, eh?" he snarled. "Well, you never made a bigger mistake in your life. I know something of wireless telegraphy myself."

Ned was conscious of nothing but a hot flame of anger that seemed to bathe him from head to foot in its fury. He flung the helmet from his head and sprang at Merritt like a tiger. Taken utterly by surprise, the fellow was carried clean off his feet by the assault. He crashed backward with Ned on top of him just as Herr Muller rushed out of Chance's cabin, waving the cipher message delightedly.

"The fleet is going to rendezvous at Blackhaven!" he was shouting. "I was right, and ———"

He stopped short as he almost stumbled over the struggling forms of Ned and Merritt. In the semi-darkness of the cabin and his excitement he had not noticed them before.

"Donnervetter, vos is diss?" he cried as he took in the situation and speedily sensed the fact that Merritt was getting the worst of the struggle.

He picked up a heavy chair that stood close to his hand. He was swinging it and was about to bring it crashing down on Ned's head when something collided with his chin.

As Herr Muller, seeing a whole constellation of stars, reeled backward, dropping the chair with a bang, he dimly realized that that "something" had been the brawny and freckled fist of one Herc Taylor.

CHAPTER XX.

NED, CAST AWAY.

But as Herc and Herr Muller crashed floorward together a rush of footsteps came down the companionway stairs. The shot that had destroyed the sending key of the sloop's wireless had been heard on deck. Rescue was at hand for the two scoundrels who had been overborne by the Dreadnought Boys.

Before hands could be laid on Herc, however, the freckle-faced youth had banged his fists twice into Herr Muller's face. He raised his hand for a third blow when a sharp pain shot through him, and he sank back with a groan of helpless pain. Something had flashed in the anarchist's hand for an instant and had buried itself in Herc's side.

"Ned! Ned!" cried the lad in accents of shrill alarm, "the fellow's stabbed me."

With a superhuman effort, Ned flung Merritt's arms from him and dashed across the cabin. Herr Muller had struggled to his feet. He rose just in time to be spun clear across the cabin by the infuriated Dreadnought Boy. Such was the force in Ned's righteously indignant blow, that before the anarchist leader ceased spinning, he crashed clear through a wooden panel.

"Herc, old fellow!" cried Ned, sinking to his knees beside his comrade, "are you badly hurt?"

"I—I—I'm all right, old chap. Save the ships!" mumbled Herc and his eyes closed. The freckled face grew fearfully white.

Before any of the excited crew could lay a hand on him Ned picked up Herc as if he had been a child, and began backing toward one of the cabin doors with him.

"You scoundrels will pay dear for this!" he shouted angrily as he went out.

Paralyzed for the time being by the lightning-like rapidity of events, not one of the men made a move just then. Ned bore Herc into the cabin unmolested. Chance, leaning on one elbow, was lying in the lower bunk. His head was bandaged, but Ned tumbled him out by the scruff of his neck.

"Out of that, you traitor!" he shouted, "and make room for a real man-o'-war's-man."

While Chance, still weak from the effects of his blow, tottered about the cabin, Ned laid Herc on the bunk as gently as a woman might have done with an infant. Herc opened his eyes and smiled up at his shipmate.

"Thanks, old fellow," he breathed, "I—I'm all right. You——"

He lapsed into unconsciousness once more.

Ned ripped his shirt open with a quick movement. With another he tore it into sheds and bandaged the wound in the lad's side. Luckily, in the struggle, Herr Muller's aim had not been good, and the knife thrust was little more than a flesh wound, extending up under Herc's armpit. But the pain was considerable.

Ned had hardly finished his work before the

men outside came out of their half-stunned period of inaction. Headed by Merritt, they charged at the cabin. Ned sprang for the door to close and lock it against them, but Chance was too quick for him. The fellow had been leaning back against the bulkhead. As Ned swept forward he extended his foot, and the Dreadnought Boy came to the floor in a heap. In another instant they were all piled on him. Ned struck out furiously.

His blows were driven by steel-plated muscles, but they had little effect on the sprawling mass of humanity piled above him. Before many minutes had passed Ned was a prisoner, tied and bound as securely as Herc had been when he was carried on board.

To his surprise, no violence was attempted by his captors. They worked in grim silence. Ned wondered vaguely what was going to happen to him. In his dazed state he didn't much care. Under Herr Muller's orders the lad was roughly

ON AERO SERVICE 217

thrust into the wireless room and the door locked upon him.

While this was being done he noted with satisfaction that upon the faces of both Herr Muller and Merritt sundry large, angry-looking swellings were beginning to obtrude themselves like purple plums.

"At any rate, I've spoiled Merritt's beauty for him," thought Ned with a grim satisfaction.

He was left unmolested in his prison place for what seemed hours. Finally, after an interminable period, he began to notice that the rough rolling motion of the sloop had ceased. Had the sea gone down, or were they at anchor in some sheltered haven, he wondered. He was not to be long in doubt.

The door was flung open. Merritt, Kennell and Muller entered. At a word from Muller the powerless Ned was shoved and half carried through the portal. Then he was propelled up the companionway stairs.

"Are they going to chuck me overboard?" he found himself wondering.

A swift glance showed him that the sloop was anchored in a small bay. The sky was clear and a bright moon showed the surroundings to be sand dunes and desolate barrens.

"Is the boat ready?" he heard Muller ask.

From over side, where the sloop's dinghy was floating, came a response in the affirmative. The next instant Ned found himself tumbled from the sloop's low side into the small craft. The fall bruised him considerably, but if his captors had expected him to make any outcry they were deceived. He uttered no word of complaint, although, what with the tightness of his bonds and the jouncing his fall had given him, he was in considerable pain.

Herr Muller, Chance, Merritt and Kennell dropped into the boat after him, taking the places of the two men who had unlimbered it from the stern davits.

Evidently their plans had been prearranged,

for Chance and Merritt fell to the oars without uttering a word. Muller and Kennell, grim and silent, sat in the stern.

It was a short row to the shore, and presently the bow of the boat grated on a sandy beach.

"Chuck him out!" growled Herr Muller.

Ned was tumbled unceremoniously out on the sands. In the moonlight he could see that the men in the boat were keeping him covered with pistols. Muller leaped out by his side.

"Keep him covered while I cut him loose," Ned heard Muller grate out.

The anarchist bent over him and severed his bonds.

"What on earth is he doing that for?" wondered Ned. But he was duly grateful as he felt his limbs free once more.

The task of cutting the ropes completed, Herr Muller lost no time in jumping back into the boat. But he need not have feared Ned, the lad was too stiff and sore to do more than feebly stretch his limbs. As soon as Muller was on board, Chance and Merritt laid hold of the bow of the boat and shoved off. They leaped nimbly on board as the little craft floated.

As they fell to their oars Muller stood up in the stern and shouted something back at Ned. The boy could not catch all of it, but he was to realize its import before long. All his ears could get of the message was something about "Island —rot there!"

Then came the rhythmic splash of oars as the boat was pulled swiftly back to the sloop. After a while Ned, although the effort made his cramped limbs wince, managed to get to his feet. He was just in time to see the sails of the sloop being hoisted and the little vessel, as they filled, stagger and move out toward the open sea once more.

"And poor Herc, wounded and alone, is on board her," was Ned's bitter thought; "but, thank goodness," he murmured the next instant, "I'm on land and free, and it won't be long before I find some means of running down that sloop."

He sat down and chafed his ankles and wrists, and after a while was able to move about freely. As soon as he did so he struck off across the sandy dunes on which he had been set ashore. A few minutes of walking brought him to a broad arm of water. It flowed swiftly under the moonlight.

A sudden flash of fear shot through Ned. He gave a slight shiver as an alarming idea shot through his mind. But he shook off his presentiment and struck out once more. It was not till he had made the third circuit of the shifting, grass-grown dunes that he realized, with a flash of horror, the bitter truth of his situation.

The inexplicable fact of his freedom and of his bonds being cast off was fully explained now.

Herr Muller had marooned the lad on a desolate island. It was cut off from the shore by a swift flowing arm of water, its current so broad and so rapid that even such a strong swimmer as

Ned did not dare trust himself to try to cross it.

By a stern effort of will Ned repressed a desire to cry aloud. Was this to be his destiny? To perish on a sandy islet off the Atlantic Coast, while the sloop forged ahead on her errand of destruction?

CHAPTER XXI

A STRIKE FOR UNCLE SAM.

How long it was that Ned sat reviewing the situation in all its bearings he never knew. But it must have been a considerable period, for, when he began to take notice of his surroundings once more, the first flush of an early summer's dawn was visible behind him as he faced what he judged to be the mainland.

The light showed the character of the country across the broad channel which separated him from it to be much the same as that of the island on which he had been marooned by the anarchists. It was criss-crossed with sand dunes till it resembled a crumpled bit of yellow parchment. Scanty, spear-like grass grew in hummocks on the undulations. As the light became stronger sea birds began to whirl about him, screaming weirdly.

Ned gazed seaward. Far out on the horizon was a smudge of black smoke. It was too great in volume for one vessel to have made. The cloud reached as far as the eye could see; as if a gigantic and dirty thumb had been swept across the sky line. To Ned it meant one thing.

"The fleet has passed down the coast on its way to Blackhaven," he mused. "Oh! for a chance to get to the mainland."

For a time he was in hopes that some fishing craft, or small boat, might pass within hail. But nothing of the kind occurred.

"I've got to get something to eat pretty soon," thought Ned, who was beginning to feel faint, "or—hullo! where have I seen that log before?"

His gaze was riveted on a big spar that was drifting idly through the arm of sea that swept between him and the land.

"I saw that fellow go through here last night; the tide must have turned and it's drifting back. Well, that settles it. There's almost as much

ON AERO SERVICE 225

water and current in there at low water as at high."

He fell to pacing the beach moodily. Once in desperation he waded into the turbid water and essayed to swim. But he was instantly swept from his feet, and a strong undertow seized on his legs and drew them down. When, panting and trembling, he stood once more on shore, he resolved not to risk his life in that manner again.

"An elephant couldn't swim that," he said to himself sadly.

All at once he looked up, from one of his despairing moods, to see something that caused him to choke and gasp with hope. Bobbing about on the water, not a hundred yards from the shore, was—of all things—a small boat!

Ned watched it fascinated.

Would the current drift it within his reach, or would it be carried tantalizingly past him? At the moment he gave little thought as to how it came to be there. It was enough for him that it was a boat, and offered—providing he could reach it—a means of getting to the mainland.

In an agony of apprehension he watched the little craft as it came on, dancing merrily on the choppy ripples of the inlet. Now it shot in toward the shore, as if it meant to drive bow-on upon the beach, and then, as Ned sprang forth to grasp it, the current would sweep it out of his reach. At last it was abreast of him, and in the next second it had passed beyond. Ned grew desperate.

"Better die in the effort to get to land than perish here of starvation and thirst," he thought.

Without bothering to kick his shoes off he sprang into the water, which was deep right up to the margin of the shore, and swam out after the boat.

In a flash he felt the undertow grip him. He struck out with every ounce of reserve strength that he possessed, but the current proved the stronger of the two. Ned, weakened by his long fast and rough experiences, found himself being rapidly drawn under.

Fighting every inch of the way he was gradually submerged. With a last effort he struck out again, but the final struggle proved too much for his already depleted muscles.

The boy was sucked under like a straw.

Where his head had appeared a second before, there was now nothing but the whirl of the waters.

Suddenly, just as it felt as if his lungs must burst, Ned was shot up to the surface once more. Too weak to strike out he flung out his hands in a desperate effort to clutch at anything to sustain his weight.

His hands closed on something solid that buoyed him up refreshingly. It was the gunwale of the boat!

Ned hung limply to her side, getting back his strength as she glided along. After several minutes he felt equal to the effort of trying to board her. He kicked his way round to the stern and clambered over the transom.

Once on board he lay languidly on the thwarts for some time, too much exhausted even to move. But by-and-bye, his strength began to trickle back. He raised himself and looked around him. About the first object his eyes lighted on was a bit of crumpled paper in the bottom of the craft.

"Maybe this is some sort of a clew as to how the boat happened along so providentially," thought Ned.

He opened the paper, scanned the few words it contained, and then his jaw dropped in sheer amazement. The words of the note were in Herc's big, scrawly handwriting.

"Ned, Hope you find the boat. I heard them say they had marooned you on an island, so I cut the rope. Herc."

Ned saw at once what had happened, even if a glance at the cut end of rope in the bow had not told him. Herc had managed to reach out of the cabin port and slash the rope by which the dinghy had been attached to the sloop's stern. It had been a long chance, but it had won out.

"I don't believe there's another chap in the world like good old Herc," thought Ned tenderly, with a suspicious mist in his eyes as he thought of his absent comrade; then he took up the oars.

"Now where shall I row to?" he asked himself, as he pulled the boat along.

He scanned the barren-looking coast, with its inhospitable sand dunes and melancholy-colored grass, with the sea birds wheeling and screaming above.

"Humph! Not much choice, apparently. I guess I'll pull just inside of that little point yonder, and then strike out across the country. I'll have to trust to luck to find somebody who'll give me a hand."

Half an hour later Ned pulled the small boat ashore and abandoned it.

When he landed he had cherished some hopes of finding a fisherman's hut, or "beachcomber's" dwelling behind the rampart of sand dunes. But no trace of even such primitive habitations met his eye. Salt meadows, threaded by muddy, sluggish creeks, lay inland, and beyond was rising ground dotted with clumps of woodland.

This looked hopeful. Determined to keep pegging along to the uttermost that was in him, Ned struck out across the salt meadows.

It was harder work than he had thought. Under the hot sun the miasmic salt land steamed and perspired. Rank odors arose, and the muddy creeks steamed. Once or twice he had to wade through the foul water courses, and, at such times myriads of bloated-looking crabs, that had been sunning themselves, scuttled, with splashes, into the water.

To add to his discomfort, as the sun grew higher, millions of black flies and stinging midges arose to plague him. They settled on him in swarms. Every time Ned wiped out a legion of the tormentors that had settled on his face, his countenance bore a red smudge. By the time he had—he hardly knew how—traversed this bad bit

ON AERO SERVICE

of country and found himself on a dusty white highroad, Ned was scarcely a presentable-looking object. Mud, from the creeks he had waded, caked his legs; his face was red and bloody from the onslaughts of the insects. His clothes were tattered from his fight on the sloop, and, altogether, he was not an object to inspire confidence.

To add to his misfortunes, he had no money, and Ned knew enough of the world to know that a lad in his condition, tattered and penniless, does not, as a rule, excite any feeling but suspicion. However, when about half a mile further on he came to a small house nestling among rose vines and creepers, he walked bravely up to the door and knocked.

A prim-looking old maid, in a checked apron, opened the door. As soon as her eyes fell on Ned she uttered a shrill scream and slammed the door with an exclamation of alarm and indignation.

"Get along with you, you tramp!" she cried.

Ned turned and trudged down the footpath.

But, as he reached the gate, he heard a commotion behind him. He turned just in time to face a big, savage-looking bulldog that was about to fly at his leg. Ned raised his foot and planted it fair and square on the snarling animal's mouth.

The dog fled with a yelp of pain. Ned followed it with his eyes.

"I'll bet that cur has fared better than I have for the last twenty-four hours," he muttered as he once more began his weary trudging along the dusty highroad.

CHAPTER XXII.

SOME ADVENTURES BY THE WAY.

By noon his hunger was positively ravenous. Yet he did not like to risk another rebuff by asking for something to eat at any of the thrifty-looking farmhouses he passed.

Of course, Ned could have represented himself as one of Uncle Sam's sailors, but it was, somehow, repugnant to him—the idea of asking for food and urging, as an excuse for the petition, the uniform he was entitled to wear and the flag he served under.

All at once as he rounded a turn in the road he came upon a scene that quickened his hunger tenfold. A group of men, women and children were bivouacked under a tree enjoying the shade, and were evidently about to enjoy a picnic lunch. Two or three buggies, and an aged carry-all stood near at hand. Ned, with averted gaze, was hurrying by, when a voice hailed him.

"Hullo, there, shipmate!"

Ned turned quickly. It was a middle-aged man, with a sunburned face, dressed in a prosperous farmer's best, who had hailed him.

"Sam Topping!" exclaimed Ned, genuinely pleased, "what are you doing here?"

"Why, picnicking, as you see. But what on earth does all this mean?" his eyes roamed over Ned's disreputable figure. "What has happened? What are you tramping about in that rig for?"

Sam Topping had served on the *Manhattan* during Ned's days as a raw apprentice. He had retired, a short time before, on a well-earned pension, and his savings had served to buy him a farm. Ned recalled now having heard that Sam had settled down in that part of the country.

The lad colored as Sam put his question. He could feel the women and children of the group looking curiously at him, while the men regarded him with more frank curiosity. It was plain that

ON AERO SERVICE 235

they looked upon him as a tramp or something of the kind. A traveling peddler, possibly.

As Sam seemed to be waiting for an answer to his question, Ned drew him aside. He told him as much of his story as he thought advisable. Sam was sympathetic. He invited Ned to lunch with them, and after the lad had washed and made himself more presentable at a small stream, he joined the party. They made him welcome, and no embarrassing questions were asked. Sam had concocted a story to fit the case while Ned was at his wayside ablutions. How good that food tasted to the half-famished boy! He could not help thinking, in the midst of his enjoyment, of poor Herc. He wondered sadly how his shipmate was faring.

With this came another thought. The safety of the fleet was imperilled. Its salvation lay in his hands. He alone could give warning of the danger that threatened from the anarchists. When he got an opportunity, he questioned the friendly Sam.

"How far is it to Blackhaven?"

"Well, let's see," rejoined Sam thoughtfully, "it's about one hundred miles to the closest point. But Blackhaven Bay, where the warships go, is twenty miles from a railroad, and only a few fishing villages are on its shores. It's a wild and desolate spot."

"I've got to get there," said Ned.

Sam looked at him as if doubtful that he was in his right mind.

"Get to Blackhaven!" he exclaimed. "What for?"

"To join my ship," explained Ned, not wishing to go into details concerning the anarchists. Sam was a talkative person, and if all he knew was noised abroad it might defeat the justice Ned was grimly determined to visit on them.

Sam had already explained the occasion of the roadside picnic. The party was composed of himself and several of his neighbors on their way into Dundertown, about five miles off, to witness a performance of the circus. Ned had already noted upon barns and outhouses as he came along the gaudy colored posters announcing its arrival. They had interested him particularly, as one flaming bill had set forth the wonderful aerial feats of one Professor Luminetti, who was modestly billed as "The King of the Air." The professor, it appeared, performed his feats in an aeroplane of similar construction to the one which Ned had been using.

"I'd like to see that chap," Ned had thought, as he regarded the pictures.

"Tell you what you do, Ned, old shipmate," quoth Sam suddenly. "You come into town with us and see the circus. There's a recruiting office in Dundertown. You can go there afterward and tell them your story. They'll probably advance you the money to get back to your ship."

Ned agreed that this would be a good idea. But he declined the circus invitation. He was too anxious, for reasons of which we know, to rejoin the fleet. The gravest danger threatened the flower of the American navy, and, for all Ned knew, its fate depended on the speed with which he could reach Blackhaven.

Soon afterward the farmers and their wives clambered into their rigs and started driving toward town. Sam, who was unmarried, drove alone, and Ned shared a seat in his buggy. It seemed to his tired frame and blistered, worn feet, the most luxurious conveyance he had ever known. Sam drove straight on to the circus lot. It presented a lively scene of shifting color and action.

Bright flags, huge erections of lumping canvas, blaring brass bands were everywhere. In front of the main tent a big crowd had gathered. Sam and Ned were caught in a swirl of humanity and rushed toward it. By a shifting of the crowd they soon found themselves in its midst. The throng was grouped about an aeroplane, the motor of which was already whirring and buzzing. By it stood a man in red tights, bright with spangles. He was lecturing on the points of the machine, which formed a "free attraction" to draw the crowds.

Ned smiled as he listened. The fellow evidently didn't know much about his subject. But even at that, he knew more than his listeners, who gazed on him, gaping and awestruck. It was the first time that most of them had seen an aeroplane at close range. The sight seemed to fascinate them.

"I will now make a short flight," announced the man as he finished, and as he clambered into the seat, a regular "barker" began shouting at the top of his voice:

"Lum-in-e-t-t-i! The King of the Ae-ar! See him in his unprecedented frantic, furious, thrilling flight into space! Watch him soar toward the haunt of the eagle bird and cloud-land! The sight of a century! The wonder of the nations! Lumin-e-t-t-i! Luminett-i-i-i-i-i! The Ke-eng of the Ae-ar!"

The crowd came running from all directions at the cry. It was soon packed so densely about "The King of the Air" that Ned and Sam found themselves almost within touching distance of the wing tips. All at once Ned's trained eye noted something. A link in one of the drive chains of the propellers was badly twisted.

Under a sudden strain it would be likely to snap.

He stepped forward and touched "The King of the Air" on the shoulder.

"Well," growled the King gruffly, "what's up?"

His gruffness was not unnatural. He saw in Ned only a rather tattered-looking member of the crowd, and *not* one of the most competent airmen of the United States Navy.

"One of the links on your drive chain is twisted," said Ned; "I thought I'd tell you."

"Oh, it is, is it?" brusquely rejoined the other; "since when have you qualified as an expert?"

"It's dangerous," Ned warned him again in an earnest voice.

"Oh, mind your own business," was the impatient reply; "it's all right, I guess. Anyhow, I'm not taking lessons from a Rube."

The crowd began to laugh and jeer. A big man in a loud check suit, and with an aggressive black moustache, came bustling up.

"Now, then! Now, then!" he exclaimed truculently. "What's up here? What do you want, young man?"

"This man's machine is not in a condition for a flight," exclaimed Ned hotly.

"Oh, it isn't, eh?" he said sarcastically. "Well, I tell you what, young man, you be off, or you'll be in no condition for a flight, either, 'cause I'll have you locked up!"

"Ho! ho! ho!" roared the crowd.

"All right. If he's injured, it will be his own and your fault," said Ned sharply.

Burning with mortification, he elbowed his way through the crowd to its outskirts. As he reached them he heard a deep-throated murmur.

"He's off!"

"Hooray!" shouted the crowd, but in a jiffy their cheering changed to a groan of dismay. There was a sharp crack like a pistol shot. The twisted link had parted under the strain of the engine, as Ned knew it would.

Luckily, the accident had happened just as the aeroplane began to move, and no damage was done to machine or aviator. Waiting only to ascertain this, Ned took his leave of Sam, and set out for the recruiting office to tell his story.

CHAPTER XXII.

"YOU ARE A PRISONER OF THE GOVERNMENT!"

He found it without much difficulty. It was located in a building in the centre of the town. The Stars and Stripes hung from the doorway. Ned saluted the flag as he passed under it. His heart beat more hopefully, and his step lightened and quickened. Already he felt as if his troubles were over.

A rather gruff-looking, red-faced quartermaster was in charge. He looked up sharply from a paper-littered desk as Ned entered.

"Well," he said quickly, "what can I do for you?"

"A good deal," rejoined Ned, and launched into his story forthwith.

"Humph!" said the man, when he concluded, "and so you want money to rejoin the fleet at Blackhaven?"

"Yes," said Ned. "I have, as I hinted, a good reason for my request. If I had had the money, I should have lost no time in communicating with Lieutenant De Frees."

"Humph! By the way, just tell me your name, young man."

"Strong—Ned Strong," rejoined Ned.

The red-faced man grew redder than ever, and burrowed among his papers like an industrious rabbit. At last he unearthed what he wanted and scanned it closely. He kept glancing from the paper to Ned, and from Ned to the paper, till the lad felt quite embarrassed. At last he finished.

"Humph!" he said, with his usual preparatory clearing of the throat, "so you are Ned Strong. It's a lucky thing you came in here, Strong."

"How is that?" asked Ned, with a smile. "Of course, I hope it's lucky for me," he added quickly.

"Humph! No, it's lucky for me," insisted the other.

"Is that so?" asked Ned, not knowing just what else to say.

The red-faced man rose to his feet, and, without another word, went into an adjoining room. Ned could hear him telephoning, but could not catch the words. He came back presently and sat down at his table once more.

"Can you advance me the money?" demanded Ned. "It's very important, you know, that I should start as soon as possible."

"Oh, yes; humph! by all means; humph! the money is on its way from the bank now."

"Thank you," said Ned simply.

"It must be a large sum," he thought to himself.

He picked up a paper that lay near at hand. Idly, to pass the time, he scanned it. Sandwiched in amidst the sensational news—for which Ned's wholesome mind did not care—was a headline that caught his eye:

"FLEET SAILS FOR BLACKHAVEN."

Ned's heart pounded violently. The recollection of that fluttering wireless message he had caught came back to him. With it, also, came a vivid remembrance of the torpedoes under the floor of the anarchists' craft.

Suddenly another item caught his eye:

"Mysterious Happening at Naval Aero Station—Two Navy Aviators Missing With Sum of Money."

All at once Ned caught his own name and then Herc's. The type swam before him for an instant, but he steadied his vision and read on. The paper gave a sensational account of their mysterious disappearance from the hotel in Bartonville. It also stated that Herc had drawn some of the money intrusted to their care just before he left.

"The men are being sought for by the department," the despatch added, "and when arrested will be summarily dealt with. Every recruiting office and naval station in the country, as well as the police, have been notified."

Ned looked up from his paper with startled eyes. He caught the gaze of the red-faced quartermaster fixed accusingly on him.

"So you've read it?" said that dignitary.

"I've read a lot of sensational rubbish," was the hot reply.

"Not half so sensational or rubbishy as what you've told me," sniffed the quartermaster.

"That being the case," said Ned hotly, "I shall not bother you further. Good afternoon."

"Hold on there! Humph! humph! Not so fast!" exclaimed the other, rising and stepping swiftly between Ned and the door, "you've to wait here a while."

"Wait!" echoed Ned. "I can't wait. Why, man alive, the safety of the fleet depends on my reaching there."

"Oh, nonsense! You don't mean to say you've brooded over that story so much you believe it yourself?"

Ned was first thunderstruck and then horrified. In living through the extraordinary events of the recent past, it had never struck him how fantastic and impossible they would seem to the average man.

"But it's true, I tell you! I can prove it, every word!" he burst out.

"How?"

"Why, by my shipmate, Hercules Taylor."

"Where is he?"

"A prisoner on that sloop."

"Come, come, young man. You've been reading too many dime novels. Why, there isn't a court martial in the land that would believe such a cock-and-bull story. I'll wager that your chum Taylor is hiding some place around town while you came up here to try and raise some more money. I must say it was a nervy thing to do."

"Good heavens!" cried Ned. "Do you mean to say that you don't credit a word of my story?"

"Nary a word. A wilder yarn I never listened

ON AERO SERVICE

to, and I've served on all kinds of craft, man and boy, for a good many years. Now, let me give you a bit of advice, young fellow. When you are on trial, don't spring any such gammoning as you've told me. Just stick to the plain truth and you may get off lighter than you otherwise would."

Ned gasped. For an instant he almost lost control of himself. But he realized that, if he was to be of service to the fleet, he must keep his self-possession.

"When I rejoin the fleet," he said, "it won't be as a prisoner."

"Won't, eh? Don't be too sure of that," was the response.

A sudden heavy tramping was heard on the stairs.

The quartermaster flung open the door.

"Here he is now," he called out, "the fellow Strong. Take him into custody and lock him up till I arrange with the naval authorities to have him sent back to his ship."

As he spoke, several heavy-footed men filed into the room. They all bore the unmistakable stamp of the country constable.

Ned's tongue almost stuck to the roof of his mouth, it grew so dry. Every nerve in his body quivered. Was it possible that all this was real? It seemed more like an ugly nightmare.

"Look here," he exclaimed, in a voice he tried to render calm and collected, "this has gone far enough. Everything can be explained. But you mustn't lock me up now. Let me go back to the fleet. There is a conspiracy on foot to destroy some of the ships. I must warn——"

A rough laugh interrupted him.

"What kind er moonshine be that, young chap?" grinned the constable. "Yer don't go ter thinkin' we puts any stock in such talk as thet, do yer? If yer do, yer mus' think we're 'dunderheads' jes 'cos this is Dundertown. Na-ow, come on! Air you comin' quiet, or air yer comin' rough?"

Ned turned to the quartermaster, who stood

pompously puffed up, surveying the civil authorities with a patronizing air.

"Remember, officer," he said, "humph! the prisoner is not a civil prisoner. He is only placed in your temporary care by me as a representative of the United States government."

"Ve-ree well," rejoined the constable; "we'll take care of him, by heck! Jes' bin pinin' ter put some 'un in ther new jail. Thet reminds me, we've got another prisoner ter pick up daown ter ther circus grounds."

"His name isn't Taylor, this chap's companion, humph?" demanded the quartermaster.

"No. It's jes' a pickpocket. We'll go by the circus on our way to ther lock-up. It's only a step out'n our way. Come on, young feller."

He extended a pair of handcuffs. Ned burned with shame and mortification. Suddenly he bethought himself of Sam and all the picnic party at the circus. What if they should see him with handcuffs on? What would they think?

"For heaven's sake," he begged, "don't put

those things on me. I'll give you my word of honor not to try to escape if you don't."

"Wa-al, I dunno," said the constable doubtfully, "handcuffs is reg-lar, but——"

"Put them on him—humph!" shrilled the quartermaster.

Luckily, this ill-natured interruption turned the tide in Ned's favor.

"Say, quartermaster," snapped the constable, "this man is er civil prisoner, fer the time being, an' what I say goes. Don't you go ter buttin' in."

"Ain't you going to put handcuffs on him?" exclaimed the naval officer.

"No, I bean't."

"I order you to."

"Keep yer orders fer ther navy. I'm constable uv this taown, an' I say this prisoner don't wear 'em."

"I'll report you to—to the president," was the tremendous threat of the pompous quartermaster, who had turned as red as an angry turkey cock.

"Even ther president of this United States

ain't a-goin' ter say ha-ow things is to be run in Dundertown," snapped the constable. He laid a hand on Ned's elbow.

"Come on, young man," he said, "you promised to come quietly, remember."

Ned turned imploringly to the quartermaster.

"You have taken the oath of allegiance to the navy," he said passionately. "Now act up to it. Find some means to warn the fleet at Blackhaven that anarchists are going to try to torpedo some of the ships. Warn them against a black sloop with a red line round her bulwarks."

"Warn them against a fiddlestick!" sniffed the quartermaster. "Who ever heard such nonsense? Humph!"

Ned almost groaned aloud as he was ushered out, with a deputy on either side of him. But he managed to control himself. The lad had been in many tight places in foreign lands, and in active service. But not one of them had been more trying to bear up under than this disaster that had befallen him in a peaceful country town in his native land.

"When will my case be heard?" Ned asked, as they reached the street. He was in hopes that if it was to come up immediately he could convince the magistrate, or whatever dignitary he was tried by, that his arrest was absolutely unjustified.

"Wa-al, squire won't be back to ta-own till day arter ter-morrer," was the reply that dashed his hopes. "Anyhow, he couldn't do nuthin' fer yer. We're only holding yer here. You're a prisoner of the United States government."

Those were the bitterest words that Ned had ever heard. They seemed to sear his very being.

CHAPTER XXIV.

A DASH FOR FREEDOM.

To Ned's intense relief, the little cortege did not attract much attention as it passed down the street. Most of the town was at the circus, attracted, doubtless, by the prospect of a big, free aeroplane flight.

At last they reached the circus grounds. The performance had commenced, and the spaces outside the tents in which it was going on were almost deserted. Only a few canvasmen and hangers-on lounged about. From time to time a loud blare of music or a shout of applause came from the tent. Over by the main entrance Ned saw Professor Luminetti, still tinkering with his aeroplane. Some men were helping him. Among them was the man with the big moustache, who had addressed Ned so roughly when he pointed out the defective link.

"There, professor," he was exclaiming, as the constable came up, "that's done. I guess everything is all right now for the night performance."

"It all came from not paying attention to what that young chap said," put in one of them.

"Yes, the professor thought he knew it all," put in another.

"Hullo! There's the young chap now," said the black-moustached man, who was the manager of the show. "Say, young feller, you're all right. Any time you want a——"

He was about to shake Ned by the hand, when the constable interposed.

"You the manager of this sheebang?"

"Yes. What of it?"

"Wa-al, I'm ther constable. Whar's that pickpocket yer telephoned about?"

"Right inside the sideshow tent. We put him in there under the guard of two canvasmen."

"All right. I'll come and git him. Two uv you boys guard the prisoner here while I'm gone."

He hastened off. Ned felt his face burn as

some of the men who had been clustered about Professor Luminetti gazed curiously at him. The word "prisoner" had attracted their attention.

The professor was too busy with his machine to pay any attention. He was starting up the engine to test it. The motor burred wildly and emitted flashes of flame and blue smoke. Suddenly he looked around.

"Say, young feller," he said to Ned, "if you know so much about aeroplanes, just tell me what ails this motor?"

Ned looked at his two guardians. They, perhaps curious to see if the lad really knew anything about air-craft, nodded permission. After all, they argued to themselves, there was no chance for the lad to escape. Ned, forgetting his troubles for a time in his joy at again being able to "fuss" over an aeroplane, bent over the refractory engine.

"The trouble's in one of the footpedals," he announced before long.

"Have to climb into the seat to fix it?" asked Luminetti.

"Reckon so."

Ned looked at his guardians. They nodded.

"Don't fly away," cried one of them jokingly, as Ned seated himself, grasped the levers and placed his foot on the pedals to test the mechanism.

"It would be a good joke if——"

Professor Luminetti, standing by the machine, was suddenly brushed off his feet and rolled over on the sward.

"Br-r-r-r-r-r-r-r-r-r-r-r-r!"

A terrific whirring, like the voice of a multitude of locusts, filled the air.

Something huge and winged and powerful flashed by the amazed deputies, and launched itself into the air. Before they recovered their wits, it was out of reach.

"It's the aeroplane! He's stolen my aeroplane!" screamed Professor Luminetti.

"Hi! Come back!" yelled the deputies.

ON AERO SERVICE 259

But so swiftly had the aeroplane shot into space that Ned was already out of ear-shot.

Hearing the babel of excited sounds, the constable came dashing from the tent. In the excitement, he let go of the pickpocket's collar, and that miscreant at once darted off.

"Get him! Bring him back!" shouted the arm of the Dundertown law.

"What do you think we are—a couple of birds?" demanded his deputies. "Get him yourself!"

The constable drew out his revolver and began firing into the air. He might as well have fired at the moon as at Ned. The aeroplane dwindled swiftly to a winged blot, then to a speck, and, finally, vanished altogether.

"I'll swear out a warrant for him!" shouted the manager.

"Well, don't do any more swearing, then," warned the constable, "er I'll arrest you fer usin' profane langwidge. I've lost two prisoners, an' I've got ter lock up somebody."

Luckily, at that moment, a small boy was captured as he was creeping under the canvas. In the act of giving him a sound spanking, the irate group left behind found some salve for their wounded feelings. Luminetti raved and tore his hair. The manager promised to wreak dire vengeance on Ned as soon as he got hold of him. As for the populace, when the story leaked out, some of them, among these being Sam, were so unfeeling as to laugh heartily. As for the quartermaster, he at once set about to report the constable to all the authorities in the United States, from the president down.

In the meantime, what of Ned?

If any of our readers imagine that he took the aeroplane on purpose, they are mistaken. What seemed like a cleverly executed plan of escape was, in reality, the result of an accident, pure and simple, but a fortunate one, as it proved.

When Ned had placed his foot on the starting pedal, to his astonishment the bit of machinery refused to budge. He pressed harder, and, suddenly something snapped. The next instant Ned felt himself being hurtled forward over the ground.

To prevent the aeroplane plunging into a tent or wagon and being wrecked, he had resorted to the only mode of procedure possible. He had set the rising planes.

Instantly the aeroplane responded. Behind him Ned could hear shouts and cries, and guessed that those he had left behind were imagining he was attempting to escape.

"If I land I'll have a hard job convincing them I wasn't," said Ned to himself.

But nevertheless, the lad tried with all his might to check the aeroplane's flight. But whatever had broken rendered this impossible. Try as he would, he could not stop the engine. His only safety, therefore, lay in keeping aloft. As the aeroplane rushed on through space, it gathered speed instead of diminishing the fury of its course.

It was all Ned could do to cling to the seat and control the frantic buckings and plungings of his aerial steed. The fact that though similar to the one he used, he was unfamiliar with the particular aeroplane in which he found himself, complicated his difficulties.

"I guess the only thing to do is to keep on till the gasolene gives out," he thought, after his twentieth attempt to check his runaway engine. "Reminds me of Don Quixote's ride with Sancho Panza to the palace of the magician in cloudland," was the whimsical thought that occurred to him. "Poor old Herc! It's not very complimentary to him to compare him to Sancho, but I wish he was here with me."

The fuel tank of the aeroplane must have been well filled, for the engine ran just as strongly at the end of an hour of aerial traveling as it had at the beginning of the trip.

"I'd turn round if I dared," thought Ned; "but I can't check the speed of the thing, and it would

ON AERO SERVICE

be suicidal to try to switch my course while going at this speed."

Ned's plight may be compared to that of a lad on a runaway bicycle on a steep hill. He did not dare turn for fear of disaster, and yet he didn't quite know what would happen if he kept on. However, he didn't have to be scared of colliding with a wagon!

Suddenly, to Ned's huge joy, the engine showed signs of slackening speed. He gently manipulated a lever, and found that he had partial control of the machine now. This being so, he decided to land as soon as practicable. From a clump of trees some distance ahead, the white spire of a church told him of a village. To his left hand lay the sea. Ned gazed at it longingly, as he dropped nearer and nearer to the ground.

He landed at the edge of a meadow adjoining a building which was occupied by the village post-office and telegraph office. A sign on a house across the way made his heart leap:

"Blackhaven Hotel."

Chance had actually brought him within close range of the fleet. It seemed too good to be true. But a crowd of villagers, who came rushing to inspect the visitor from cloudland, soon put all other thoughts but the safety of his machine out of his mind. If he had not watched it carefully, there seemed to be danger of its being ripped to bits by souvenir hunters.

A brief inspection showed Ned that a broken tension-spring had caused the runaway. It was soon adjusted. Then he peeped into the gasolene tank. It was almost empty.

"They sell gasolene in ther store there, mister," said a bright lad. "Gasolene gigs come through here onct in a while."

"When they's lost," struck in another lad.

This was good news to Ned. Leaving the lads to guard the machine, he entered the post-office. The postmaster imperturbably sold him five gallons of gasolene. Ned recollected that he couldn't pay for it. But, unfortunately, this did not occur to him till he had emptied it into the tank.

ON AERO SERVICE 265

Hardly had he done so, and was starting back to the store with explanations, when the postmaster, who was also telegraph operator, appeared in the doorway of his emporium. He was waving a yellow telegram.

"Hold that feller, one of yer!" he shouted. "That thar's a stolen sky-buggy, and he's no better than a thief!"

A dozen men started forward to lay hands on Ned.

But a sudden determination had come to the lad. He was within striking distance of the fleet. It was his duty to warn the officers of the peril that menaced their vessels.

A rough hand seized his arm. Ned flung it off. At the same instant his fists drove full at a big fellow—the village blacksmith—who tried to bar his path, swinging a heavy hammer.

"Stand clear!" shouted Ned, as he sprang into the seat of his machine—or rather Professor Luminetti's—"this machine isn't stolen—*it's borrowed on Uncle Sam's service!*"

The next instant the machine skyrocketed upward, leaving behind it a trail of smoke, and sensation that furnished talk for the village of Blackhaven for more than a year.

CHAPTER XXV.

THE MYSTERIOUS SCHOONER—CONCLUSION.

"Bulkley, do you see some object in the air—off there to the northwest?"

Commander Dunham, of the Dreadnought *Manhattan,* paused in his steady pacing of the after deck, and turned to Ensign Bulkley, the officer of the deck.

Ensign Bulkley brought into play the insignia of his diurnal office, a powerful telescope, done in brown leather, with polished, black metal trimmings. With it, he swept the sky in the direction indicated by his superior, for some minutes.

"I do see something, sir," he said presently, "a black object, like a large bird. But it's bigger than any bird I ever saw. By Jove, sir, it's—it's an aeroplane!"

"An aeroplane! Impossible. How could one

find its way to Blackhaven Bay? And what could be its errand here?"

"I've no idea, sir. But I'll wager my commission that it is one. Suppose you look yourself, sir?"

The officer of the deck handed his telescope to his commanding officer. Commander Dunham gazed intently through it for a few moments. Then he turned to Bulkley.

"By all that's wonderful, you're right, Mr. Bulkley. It seems to be coming this way, too."

"Not a doubt of it, sir. But at the rate it is advancing it should not be long before we are aware of its errand."

"At all events, it will relieve the montony, Bulkley. Anchored here since yesterday and no orders yet. However, I suppose mine practice and general gunnery will be the program."

"I expect so, sir," was the response.

Both officers gazed over the leaden expanse of the landlocked bay about them.

Five battleships, two cruisers, and three torpedo-boat destroyers lay at anchor, in regular files. Hard by was a "parent ship," with her flotilla of submarines nestling alongside, like small chickens round a motherly old hen.

"Desolate country hereabouts," said Commander Dunham presently. "I shouldn't have thought that an airman could have found his way here."

"It hardly seems possible," agreed his junior; "it's as barren a bit of coast as can be imagined."

The aeroplane drew closer. Its outlines were quite apparent now. On every vessel of the fleet excitement over its approach was now visible. Bright bits of bunting began to "wig-wag" the news from ship to ship. On every foredeck jackies almost suspended the tasks in hand to watch the oncoming of the aerial craft.

"What a contrast, Bulkley," observed Commander Dunham presently. "See that old sloop off there to seaward? She is of an almost obsolete type, while above us is coming the herald of a new era in peace, as well as war."

"That is so, sir. But that sloop, obsolete as she may appear, is quite fast. I understand she has been tacking about the fleet all day. I wonder what she wants?"

"Some fisherman, probably. However, see that she does not come too close. In confidence, Bulkley, I have been warned, in common with every other commander of the fleet, to beware of a band of daring anarchists who, it appears, have made no secret abroad of their intention to damage the United States navy."

The navy officer showed no surprise. It is a common enough incident for warnings of the same character. The mail of the navy department at Washington is always full of letters—some of them menacing in tone—from over-zealous apostles of "universal peace." Occasionally, too, a spy is unearthed serving in Uncle Sam's uniform. Such fellows are usually deported quietly and swiftly.

"I shall keep an eye on that sloop, sir, in that

case," said the ensign, "but I'm afraid it will be difficult to do so before very long."

"How is that, Bulkley?"

The ensign waved his hand seaward. A hazy sort of atmosphere enveloped the horizon.

"Fog, eh?" commented the commander.

"Yes, sir. It will be all about us soon, or I'm mistaken. But look, sir, that aeroplane is almost above us."

"By George!—so it is. What's the aviator doing? He's signalling us. He's pointing downward, Bulkley, too."

"Looks as if he wanted to land on our decks, sir."

"It does. Hark! What's that he's shouting? Pshaw, I can't hear. Tell you what, Bulkley, order the aerial landing platform rigged at once. It ought not to take more than fifteen minutes."

"I'll have it done at once, sir."

The officer hastened off on his errand. A scene of bustle ensued. A hundred jackies were busy transporting sections of the adjustable platform on which Ned had landed on the occasion of his great triumph. The scene appeared to be involved in inextricable confusion. But each man had his task to perform, and each pursued it industriously. Before long the platform was up— all but the flooring. The work of laying this on the steel uprights and skeleton supporting structure was soon accomplished.

All this time the mysterious aerial visitant had been hovering aloft. But his task of keeping above the battleship was getting momentarily more and more difficult. The atmosphere was rapidly thickening. In white wraiths and billows the fog, which Ensign Bulkley had prophesied, came rolling in. Beads of moisture gathered on everything. From the deck the tops of the basket-like military masts grew every minute more difficult to espy. The aeroplane, circling in space, was a mere blur.

"All ready, sir," announced Ensign Bulkley before long. By this time the after-deck was crowded with officers. All were gazing upward into the steamy fog.

"Give him a signal, Bulkley," ordered the commander.

"He'll find it hard to see one, sir."

"Signal the bridge, then, to blow three blasts on the siren. He can hear that."

"Hoo-oo-o-o-o! Hoo-oo-o-o-o! Hoo-o-o-o-o!"

A few seconds later the uncanny voice of the siren cut the mist. Without hesitation, the dim object in the fog above them, began to come downward. It swung through the thick air rapidly. In a short time it was off the stern of the *Manhattan,* and ten minutes after the signal had sounded Ned Strong ran his aeroplane upon the landing platform so speedily erected.

But if the manner of his arrival had been sensational, the effect it created was even more so.

"It's Strong! The man we were wirelessed had decamped with part of Lieutenant De Frees' funds!" exclaimed Captain Dunham amazedly.

Ned half staggered from his seat and came

toward him. The sailors stood to one side, in a half-awed fashion. Ned's face, after his long and trying strain, was ghastly. His eyes shone with an unnatural brightness.

"Well, my lad," said the commander briskly, "what is the meaning of all this?"

"I—I—can I speak——" began Ned.

But suddenly the decks and the eager faces about him seemed to join in a mad dance. He swayed weakly, and would have fallen, had not some jackies near at hand caught him.

"Send that man to the sick bay," ordered Commander Dunham. "There's something out of the ordinary in all this," he said in a lower tone to his officers.

Ned was half-carried, half-supported, to the ship's hospital. He soon recovered from his temporary weakness, and asked to see the doctor at once. When that dignitary responded to the summons, he drank in, with eager ears, Ned's astonishing story. The result was, that Commander Dunham was at once requested to visit the sick bay. A conference ensued, which lasted till almost dark. By that time Ned was fully recovered.

It was after dark that a torpedo-boat destroyer, with Ensign Bulkley in command, slipped away from the fleet and vanished in the fog. On the conning tower, beside the officer, was Ned Strong.

The powerful searchlight cut a bright path through the mist ahead. Somewhere in that smother lay the craft they were in search of, the anarchists' sloop, on board of which Herc was a prisoner. How eagerly Ned longed for the fog to lift, may be imagined. But they cruised all night without a sign of its lifting. By daylight they were some distance out at sea. When, at eight o'clock, the fog began to lift, the shore was revealed, before long, as a dim, blue streak in the distance.

But nobody had eyes for that when a sudden shout went up from the lookout forward.

The man had sighted a sail on the horizon. But

as they drew closer to it, the craft was seen to be a schooner with a short, stumpy mizzen-mast.

"That's not our boat," said the ensign disappointedly.

"But what can have become of the sloop, sir?" wondered Ned. "Surely, she couldn't have vanished from sight during the night. She's not a fast enough sailer for that."

"True," said Bulkley. "By Jove!" he exclaimed suddenly, "you don't think those chaps have disguised her, do you?"

"They might have, sir. Don't you think it's worth while to board that schooner, anyhow?"

"I do, Strong," agreed the officer.

The destroyer was headed toward the schooner. The wind had dropped and the vessel was rolling idly on the oily sea.

"Aboard the schooner there!" cried the officer, as they came up close to the vessel with the peculiar-looking after-mast. "Stand by! We are going to board you."

A bearded man stood at the helm. He was the

only person visible. Ned scrutinized his face eagerly, but could not recognize him. This individual only waved a hand in response to the officer's order. But, as the destroyer's way was checked, and she lay idly on the waves, he suddenly vanished into the cabin. The next instant a square port at the schooner's bow was swung open, and, without the slightest warning, a long, shining, cylindrical object was shot forth.

It struck the water with a swirl of spray, and then, with a line of white wake, in its swift course, headed straight for the destroyer.

"A torpedo!" exclaimed the officer, who, with Ned, was just about to clamber into one of the lowered boats.

The men on board set up a horrified shout. So short was the distance between the two craft that between the launching of the torpedo and the dreaded impact of its "war head" against the side of the destroyer seemed but an instant. It was a fearful instant, though, and lived long in the recollection of those who endured it.

The torpedo struck the side of the destroyer with a metallic clang. But no explosion followed. Instead, the implement floated harmlessly off.

"Phew!" exclaimed the officer, wiping his forehead. "What an escape! I thought we were all booked for Kingdom Come. Come, lads, man the oars quickly. We'll get those anarchistic rascals out of their rat-holes and make them suffer for this outrage. But what the dickens was the matter with that torpedo?" he muttered.

"I think I can explain, sir," rejoined Ned.

"By Jove, you can? Let's hear your explanation."

"You see, sir," said Ned, "while Herc and I were exploring that cabin, we found those torpedoes. Well, when an opportunity presented itself, I unscrewed the head of each, and withdrew the gun-cotton. But I was afraid that, after they marooned me, the anarchists might have examined them and found out what I'd done and reloaded them. But I'm confident now that they haven't."

"No, you've drawn their teeth with a vengeance. I tremble to think, though, what would have happened if they had had an opportunity to use one of the loaded ones. They're a sharp outfit of tricksters, too, with their disguised sloop."

"But not sharp enough to fool Uncle Sam," exclaimed Ned, as the boat was run alongside.

As it scraped the disguised sloop's side, a figure suddenly appeared on the deck. It was Herc. He made a flying leap for the boat, and landed in a heap in their midst.

"Row for your lives!" he yelled. "That maniac, Muller, is about to blow up the vessel. I got away by knocking a couple of the crew galley-west."

"Give way, men!" shouted the officer, and willing arms pulled the boat from the schooner's side. But the explosion did not come. Instead, two figures, recognized as those of Merritt and Chance, appeared on the deck. They signalled for the boat to come closer.

"We captured Muller, just as he was about to blow up the sloop," they shouted. "If we surrender, will you show us clemency?"

"I'll make no promises," was the grim reply of Ensign Bulkley.

Something like an hour later, the destroyer, with the disguised sloop in tow, re-entered Blackhaven Bay. On board her—a raving maniac—was Herr Muller. His long-smouldering insanity had at last broken into flame. He was confined on board the *Manhattan* for a time and then removed to an asylum, where he now is. He will never recover his reason, and unceasingly imagines that his mission is to destroy the United States navy. As for his followers, they received various terms in prison. Kennell, alone, escaped. It transpired that he had been sent ashore after supplies, and so was not on board the disguised sloop when the futile attempt to blow up the destroyer was made.

Of course, the suspicion which had been directed against Ned and Herc was speedily explained away, and they were rated higher than ever in the estimation of their officers. Part of the substantial monetary reward Ned received for his courage and resource in reaching the fleet, via aeroplane, was sent to Professor Luminetti, the King of the Air. The quartermaster at Dundertown received a severe reprimand for his over-zealousness, but nothing more was done to him, as, after all, he thought he was performing his duty.

Had we space, we would like to relate the further aerial adventures of Ned and Herc on Aero Service. But sufficient have been related here to convey some idea of the importance of such an adjunct to our navy. It will always be a proud boast of the Dreadnought Boys that they helped to establish the aeroplane as a valuable auxiliary of the modern battleship.

But the scenes shift rapidly on the stage of naval life. Fresh places and opportunities were shortly to be presented to the Dreadnought Boys|

Uncle Sam's navy was on the eve of its epoch-making, globe-circling voyage. If you care to follow further the careers of The Dreadnought Boys, and learn how they conducted themselves amidst novel surroundings and changing and exciting conditions, you will find it all set down in the next volume of this series, *"The Dreadnought Boys' World Cruise."*

THE END.